DIVERSION

A Mark Rollins Adventure

This is a work of fiction. While some of the names, characters, places, and incidents are products of the author's imagination and some are real, the events depicted herein are entirely fictitious and should not be considered real or factual.

Copyright ©2017 by M. Thomas Collins
All rights reserved.

ISBN: 978-1-939285-90-4 (Hardcover Edition)
ISBN: 978-1-939285-95-9 (Paperback Edition)
ISBN: 978-1-939285-92-8 (eBook Edition)

Library of Congress Control Number: 2017908576
Published by I-65 North, Inc.

Visit www.tomcollinsauthor.com.
Cover Design by Tom Trebing.

Also by M. Thomas (Tom) Collins

Mark Rollins' New Career & the Women's Health Club
Mark Rollins and the Rainmaker
Mark Rollins and the Puppeteer
The Claret Murders, a Mark Rollins Adventure
The Language of Excellence
Marion Collins Remembers Old Sayings and Lessons for Life
My Journey—Alice Elsie Welch Collins

DIVERSION

A Mark Rollins Adventure

by
TOM COLLINS

Acknowledgement

The Mark Rollins series was inspired by my daughter's stories as an aerobics instructor in one of Nashville's upscale communities. The idea for Diversion *sprang from two separate events—first, a news story about the theft of storm drains to buy drugs, and second, the growing national concern surrounding the abuse of opioid prescription pain medications.*

O God, that men should put an enemy in their mouths to steal away their brains! (Cassio, Act II, Scene iii)

—William Shakespeare, *Othello*

Prologue

I am Mark Rollins. Senior citizen. My driver's license lists my height as five feet nine inches. Eyes blue, hair brown. I'm a cancer survivor with a military-style buzz cut—a concession to chemo I exercise regularly to look younger than my years. I gave up fads eons ago and adopted my trademark uniform—khaki trousers, black cotton polo, and Cole Haan driving shoes. I drink martinis straight up with an olive, which I prefer on the side to avoid contamination by excessive juice. I prefer Skyy or Belvedere vodka. I am also in the fortunate position of having wealth and access to people in high places. Money, for me, is little more than numbers on a computer screen—numbers that keep getting larger.

My access to influential people and a penchant for adventure began in the early 1990s when the US government asked me to help fledgling tech enterprises in Eastern Europe. Our government had decided it was in our national interest to encourage emerging technology in that part of the world. Unfortunately, governments outside the West feared technology in private hands—especially with the prevalence of the Internet. Start-up businesses were also at risk of infiltration by criminal gangs. More than once, my wife, Sarah, and I became the targets of less-than-upright people. It took more than my know-how and courageous Eastern European entrepreneurs to advance global technology in that part of the world. It also required access to powerful US government forces to crush those who would prevent or preempt its advance.

After my investments in emerging technology industries paid off in a big way, I intended to retire. To my surprise, those retirement plans were derailed when I became the owner of the Women's Health Club located in the Brentwood suburb of Nashville, Tennessee. The WHC is an elite, ladies-only facility for the socially prominent and wealthy. The members work hard to maintain youthful, seductive figures. But there is more to the WHC than its glitterati clientele. It also provides cover for a highly profitable, clandestine high-tech operation—useful to any number of government agencies because of its ability to operate beyond congressional oversight. Let's just say we aren't limited by the same rules, but we never overtly break the law.

Chapter 1

The Thing

Raymond Miller, "Ray" to former friends, once thought of himself as a dashing young doctor. An anesthesiologist. He and his partner, Yusuf Arian, opened their clinic in New England. Things went well in the beginning, but there was the lawsuit—a back operation that went wrong. Rods broke and the patient died on the operating table during the corrective surgery. It wasn't Ray's fault. The rods weren't supposed to break and the patient sure as hell wasn't supposed to stop breathing. Ray had simply drunk too much at a party the night before an early-morning operation. There was a police roadblock on the way home. The local cops were looking for drunk drivers and, in Ray, they found one. It didn't take the patient's family long to find out about the DUI. It was downhill from there. He started gulping down tramadol to take the edge off, but he soon settled on his drug of choice: Scotch, and Irish whiskey. Eventually good ole bourbon—Tennessee or Kentucky. After a while, any booze would do. If bourbon wasn't available, gin, vodka, tequila, or even rum worked well enough.

Ray had managed to save his medical license, but hospital privileges were another matter. He settled into the prescription-writing business. There were no hospitals, no Medicare, and no insurance companies to contend with. It was all cash and people lined up every morning, even before the doors opened, with their phony complaints—from sciatica to migraine headaches. All they wanted was a prescription. Most of them just asked for Percocet. Serious addicts asked for OxyContin, Oxyfast, or Roxicodone. Then there were those whose doctors had cut off their supply of tramadol or Lortab—hydrocodone. A few shooters wanted fentanyl that could be mined for a syringe shot. Ray soon learned that some were willing to give him more than cash. That's when he came up with the idea of putting a bed in one of the adjoining examining rooms for "power naps." If the patient was young and female, all it took for her to get a couple of extra prescriptions was a short stint on his new bed.

As his interest in booze increased, however, his interest in sex decreased. His "bedroom" became his sanctuary when he was too drunk to drive home—a frequent occurrence. As far as his wife and family were concerned, they no longer wanted him home—ever.

The once handsome young doctor slowly disappeared, replaced by someone or some*thing* very different. Maybe it was the tramadol, the lawsuit, or the booze. He became hurtful. It wasn't bitterness; more like sadistic meanness. He wanted to cause pain. Emotionally hurt people. Prevent them from obtaining the very thing they wanted most. If he could destroy a dream, ruin a plan, or break a heart, he would. The more he drank, the worse he became. He wanted people to come crawling to him—begging. He enjoyed having people dangling on his hook. But that was before the booze took over. He was once a formidable foe. Now he was just a disgusting fool, delusional enough to still think he was smarter than everyone. He still thought he could play his power games and win.

The only things that were winning, however, were his weight, his slovenliness, his smell, which by nightfall filled his makeshift bedroom with the odor of whisky and urine. Somehow, he still managed to pull himself together in the mornings. But by 3:00 p.m., his shaky hands made signing prescriptions difficult. When the door closed on that last patient, the bottle he kept in his desk was usually empty. In the old days, to celebrate the day's last patient, he would open the clinic's well-stocked bar. In party mode, the ice bucket and tongs replaced his pen and prescription pad. He became a happy bartender offering drinks on the house to any of the nursing staff willing to stay and drink with him. Now, he just withdrew to his bedroom office with a new bottle.

Tonight he lay face down on his office bed, passed out, wearing nothing but his briefs and socks. His clothes were in a twisted pile on the floor. An almost-empty bottle of Jack Daniels was on the nightstand. A glass lay on its side on the linoleum in a pool of spilled bourbon. He was snorting like the pig he resembled. There was spittle on the pillow and little bubbles on his lips.

The doctor was a revulsion—an offense to God—a "thing" that needed to be removed. The visitor wasn't there by accident. This was planned, carefully considered. The thing on the bed would die in his drunken stupor. It would look like an overdose—booze mixed with drugs.

The visitor planned to watch and wait until it was over. No risk, no failure. No leaving until the pulse stopped—until that fat slob was stone-cold dead. Whatever it took, he would never stand in the way again. The visitor smiled at the thought of being Death calling on his victim, the Thing, and said to the unconscious slob, "Death has arrived, you asshole, and I'm sending you to hell where you belong."

Death opened the box and took out five packs. Each held a 75 mcg/h fentanyl patch. Under normal conditions, the transdermal patch is designed to deliver 75 micrograms of fentanyl per hour. Tonight's conditions, though, were not going to be normal. Death carefully tore open the first package. All the material had to be removed—incriminating evidence that must disappear. After removing the slippery thin plastic pieces that sandwiched the patch, there were still two pieces protecting the sticky side of the fentanyl. Death removed the larger piece and slid it into the opened package, then held the patch by the very tip of the exposed sticky side until the remaining small piece of plastic was removed. The Thing never felt the patch secured to his naked back. It did not stir. The Thing continued to snort and drool in his drunken stupor. Death repeated the process four more times. The Thing now wore five fentanyl patches. Death tore open another full box and added five more patches to the doctor's skin—the last two conspicuously on the shoulder where the prostrate man might have placed them himself.

Now there was ten times the normal dose attached. Fentanyl is fifty to one hundred times more potent than morphine. Death knew this. Each patch was designed to have its powerful opioids absorbed through the skin over three days. Just to be sure, though, Death intervened. All it took to speed up the absorption rate was heat. That is what the heating pad was for. It was overkill, but Death wanted it to be foolproof. Every organ would shut down. Go to sleep. As would the Thing itself.

Two hours later the snorting stopped. Dr. Raymond Miller's chest no longer rose or fell with each breath. Death removed the eight patches from around his victim's spine, then cleaned the doctor's fat back to make sure there was no residue from the adhesive. The shoulder patches remained to explain the presence of fentanyl, if anyone looked for it. Death checked one more time to be sure. There was no pulse. The Thing was dead.

CHAPTER 2

Drug Twins

Lena and Carlos De La Cruz were twins, but you wouldn't know it by looking at them. Lena had her mother's light mocha coloring and, like her mother, fiery red hair—though neither was naturally redheaded. She was tall for a Cuban woman, and thin. In her stilettos, she stood two inches taller than her brother, Carlos, who had a swarthy complexion, greasy coal-black hair, and was never seen without his aviator sunglasses.

Their grandparents had fled from Castro to become successful merchants within the Cuban community of southern Florida. It was their father, however, who brought the family permanently out of Little Havana by clawing his way into Miami social circles. He was a prominent commercial builder during a period of enormous growth and skyrocketing real estate values. He made a lot of money for his wealthy investors, many of whom were snowbirds from New York and New Jersey—a mixture of Jewish intellectuals and Italian Catholics. They liked making money. They did not like losing it. Luckily, times were on the twins' father's side. You could hardly lose dealing in Florida real estate. Lena and Carlos grew up living the good life. Daddy imposed no rules. They lived like pampered adults long before they could even drive.

In 1999, the twins' father and mother died in a private plane crash that left the twins with twelve million dollars after estate taxes. It was a good start, but for Lena and Carlos twelve million dollars wouldn't last long. Neither knew anything about the construction business. They did, however, have an enormous appetite for designer clothes, flashy cars, fast boats, expensive planes, elaborate houses, large parties, and wealthy friends. They grew up in an atmosphere where rules didn't apply to them. They shared a sense of invulnerability, of being untouchable. Rules were for other people, not them. They were fearless. Getting involved in the southern Florida drug trade came naturally. There were people with the stuff and people who wanted the stuff. So, they bought from one and sold to the other. Simple.

Lena handled the procurement and money laundering side. She was the smart one. Carlos was the muscle and handled distribution and territory management. That meant cracking a few bones when anyone tried to compete. They were making a lot of money, but the business experience taught Lena three things. First, dealing illegal drugs and cleaning up the money was arduous, never-ending work. It was cramping her style. Second, suppliers of illegal drugs were dangerous people, especially the Iranians. Third, and most important, she discovered *legal* drugs. Why deal in illegal drugs when you could make even more money selling pharmaceuticals? That's when Lena came up with the idea for Good Comfort Pain Management.

Lena and Carlos would be the legitimate investors. There was nothing illegal about investing, and if one of their pain clinics engaged in illegal activity, it would be the hired doctors who would take the legal hit. Florida was a perfect base of operation. The business conditions were right. Medical clinics, including those specializing in pain management, faced few regulations. There was a ready market. Florida was already a haven for elderly retirees with lots of aches and pains. The concentration of older citizens and Florida's lifestyle had also attracted an overabundance of licensed medical professionals to the state. It wasn't hard to find doctors who were more interested in their income than the Hippocratic Oath.

It was a perfect setup—a cash-only business. No chance of running afoul of the Feds for Medicare fraud. There was no need to launder money if you were willing to pay taxes and, of course, Lena and Carlos were. All you needed was a storefront and a doctor willing for a cash fee to write a prescription for any variety of euphoria-inducing opioids such as codeine, fentanyl, OxyContin, hydrocodone, or the family of antipsychotic and mental health drugs such as aripiprazole, ziprasidone, or risperidone.

By 2005, the twins were operating ten clinics in southern Florida alone. Each clinic saw between two hundred and three hundred patients a day. Even with its ready market, Florida provided less than a quarter of their customers. The rest came from out of state—as far away as New England, but the majority came from Tennessee,

Kentucky, and Indiana. Clinic doctors were taking home anywhere from two million to two and a half million dollars per year. But the big money went to the twins. Lena and Carlos were pocketing more than ten million dollars per clinic per year.

Florida became increasingly concerned about the state's "pill mills," but under current laws, there was little officials could do. If one of the clinics ran into problems with a regulator, managers hired by the investors blamed the doctor. They would satisfy the state's concern by firing the offending MD. The investors would replace him or her with another willing prescription writer and return to business as if nothing had happened. The "fired" doctor would be rotated to one of the twins' other holdings. Salaried doctors provided the perfect insulator between the investor twins and the law.

By 2008, however, Florida was closing the loopholes that had turned the Sunshine State into the happy pill dispenser for the eastern seaboard. The twins had to move closer to their markets.

Something else was happening as well. Something with Lena. She was aging too fast. She felt threadbare and haggard. She spent more and more time dealing with business and less and less time in her favorite South Beach nightclubs among the rich, famous, beautiful people of Miami.

Chapter 3

Lena's Mortality

Lena De La Cruz and Fares Bishara sat across from each other at a small round table for two on the veranda of the Miami De La Cruz mansion. There was a breeze coming off the water of Biscayne Bay. It was later in the day and the low, western sun sparkled on the water and lit up the colorful spinnakers of nearby sailboats. They were sharing the white wine Bishara had brought with him, Lena's current favorite, a bottle of Chateau Haut-Brion Blanc—vintage 2009.

Fares had been a top doctor in his home country, but in the United States he was unlicensed. What doctoring he did now was within a tight circle of people who didn't care about a US medical license and had no need for insurance. He had been Lena's lover, not her doctor, until he recognized the symptoms. That's when he took over her medical care. Tonight, Fares was talking to her as a doctor—as frankly but as tenderly as he knew how.

She knew this conversation was coming. Lena was aware of her body and of the symptoms. She had watched Fares's face when he brought them up, and she had looked up Eisenmenger syndrome, the medical condition he had named. She just wasn't fully prepared to face her new physical reality.

"Lena, your body is slowly being starved to death for lack of oxygen," he said. "If we had found this earlier, an operation could have taken care of it. It wouldn't have been simple, but we know how to address it. Today this is something doctors catch at birth. We typically repair the heart defect while the patient is still an infant."

"If an operation will fix this, let's get it done," said Lena as she took a deep breath.

"I'm afraid it's too late," said Fares quickly. "The damage is done. It's irreversible. Repairing the defect will not undo the damage to your heart and lungs. And now the only option is a heart-lung transplant; and in your case, there's a good chance you will need a kidney as well."

Fares knew that without the transplants, Lena would die. It could happen today, a week from now, or she could have a couple of years left. The longer it went on, the more damage to her other organs. Eisenmenger syndrome can also lead to uncontrolled bleeding and, paradoxically, the hyperviscosity of her blood could result in random blood clots that could kill her.

"Okay, if that's what it takes, then I'm ready," said Lena. "I want to go to the best hospital and have the best surgeon. It's my only life, so money doesn't matter."

"I wish it were that simple," said Fares. "You have to get in line for a heart and lung. There are laws that spell out the process. It's all handled by the federal government's OPTN, the Organ Procurement and Transplantation Network. I'm afraid your chances of getting a heart and lung in time are pretty slim."

Lena rubbed her temples and stared at the boats floating through Biscayne Bay.

"Why?" she asked, getting up defiantly and walking away from the table. "I don't understand."

"Among other things, including your lifestyle, you have Type O negative blood."

"That's good, right?" she asked, turning back toward him with a hint of hope in her voice. "They tell me I'm a universal blood donor."

"It's good if you're donating blood or organs," said Fares. "People with Type O blood can donate blood or organs to any blood type. That's why they call you a universal donor. Unfortunately, the reverse isn't true. Type Os can only receive blood and transplants from others with the same Type O blood."

"And that's a problem?"

"Yes, I'm afraid it is," he said. "Only 7 percent of the population is Type O negative. And, it gets worse. There are only twenty-six actual transplant donors per million people in the population. That percentage is tiny. Only one or two of those donors out of a million people will have Type O negative."

"Those don't sound like very good odds."

"They're not," he said. "Type O negative recipients might as well be at the back of the line—at least that's the effect of a limited supply and the current rationing rules."

Lena said nothing for several minutes. Neither did Fares. He was giving her time to take it all in. She was way ahead of him in dealing with her mortality. He was diagnosing—talking about the disease. She was already working on staying alive. She was processing it like all the other obstacles that had stood between her and what she wanted. Now she wanted to live. She was looking for the loopholes—ways to get around the rules. Money or muscle had always worked for her. You could buy away problems or use force to eliminate them. Her own mortality was the biggest obstacle Lena had ever faced. She had money and she was willing to do anything it would take to live.

Lena looked across the table at Fares, studying his face. To her it was an exotic face—big, dark eyes that seemed to sparkle under naturally arched eyebrows that any woman would die for. His nose was long and straight. His face would have come to a sharp point at the chin if it hadn't been interrupted by a deep dimple. It was also the face of a man she knew had expensive tastes. A man who liked to be around others who shared those tastes. Yes, he was like everyone else, she decided. He wanted the same things.

Finally, she spoke. "Fares, you're not a rich man, are you?"

"You know I'm not."

"Don't you want to be?"

"That's a strange question."

"No, it's a desperate question," she said. "I can make you rich. You can save my life."

"I wish I could, but there are rules," he said. "There is no way to get you to the front of the line."

"Isn't there? You know as well as I do, there are always loopholes. There are *always* ways around the rules. I will pay you five million dollars to find the loopholes and save my life."

The air on the veranda seemed to stand still. Fares paused, staring at Lena.

"That's ridiculous," he said.

"No, it's not," she said briskly. "It's life or death for me and I know there's a way. Maybe not in this country. But it's a big world. I know kidneys have a way of showing up under the radar in developing countries. What if I had a donor, either willing or not? There's got to be some surgeon somewhere in this world who would save my life for the right price. If we can't do it on land, what about in international waters—at sea?"

"That's crazy," said Fares.

"No, it's an opportunity," said Lena with a smile. "An opportunity for you to become rich, Fares Bishara."

Chapter 4

Carlos's Bad Deal

Carlos wasn't happy to be wrenched away from the Tunnel, Boston's new night spot, by a phone call from his sister. But when Lena called, he left his clubbing friends—including a shapely redhead named Julia who giggled every time he talked—and took a taxi to the airport. The idling company plane wasted no time taking off and heading south to Miami. When he landed, Lena had a helicopter waiting for him. It was a short hop to the De La Cruz mansion on Star Island where big sister was waiting. He knew what it was about.

A clinic in some small town outside Boston had never made business sense to Lena. Their kind of industry needed politicians and regulators who found it in their best interest to keep the twins' clinics open. It took time and money to build that kind of organization. It was done by spreading money around and by becoming the gatekeeper for the right social circles. Lena understood that haphazard and scattered growth would be too difficult to manage. There would be too many different jurisdictions, too many rules and regulations, and too many politicians to pay to look the other way. They needed a better strategy.

Her plan was to open new clinics in small rural areas of Tennessee. New England was too far away from their center of operation. It would be too easy to get busted for stupidity—breaking some rule or regulation without the contacts to fix it. Lena didn't have any Boston politicians in her camp like she did in Miami. She didn't know who was who in the business. She knew she wouldn't have tolerated an interloper moving into her territory. She didn't know whose toes they would be stepping on by moving into the Boston area. She didn't want to start a war.

Carlos didn't listen, didn't care. He had pressed on without her. His friends in Atlantic City wanted him to do the deal so they could collect on the gambling debts of one of the doctor owners. They were not people Carlos wanted to disappoint. His sister didn't understand. It was a macho thing. Carlos had said, "Look, we got one doctor in the bag (the gambler), and the other doctor's wife is pushing him to make the deal. I think she's looking for a way out. Ten to one says she'll grab their share of the money and run. This is an easy deal—too easy to let slip through our fingers. I can make this happen. And that, sister, would make our friends very happy."

Before Lena could stop things, her opposition was derailed. The reluctant partner turned up dead and the deal was in motion without her. Like it or not, the twins now owned the Pain Management Center of Quincy, a small township outside Boston. Very quickly, Lena's concern about their lack of influence in the area proved prophetic.

The death of the reluctant partner was drawing too much attention. Massachusetts was too far away from Florida for the twins to extend their political influence. The partner's death was too fortuitous for Lena's liking. It wasn't her style.

"Get off my back, sis," said Carlos as he poured himself a drink in their Star Island mansion. "They say he killed himself, so why do you keep nagging me about this? I didn't off the guy!"

Lena wasn't buying Carlos's feigned innocence. Even if he had no direct role in the man's death, someone he had connections with probably did. That could lead back to her.

"You know damn well that the suicide thing may not hold up," said Lena. "If people smell a rat, and reporters keep digging, the police may reopen the case."

"There's no dead rat—no smell," said Carlos. "There's no reason for them to reopen anything, sis."

"Oh no?" she snapped. "Think about it, Carlos. There's your connection to Atlantic City. The Feds know about their middleman role involving Middle East drug suppliers. They aren't your friends, Carlos. The authorities are always looking for something they can hang on people working with those guys. That puts us at risk."

Carlos paused before he spoke, stroking his cleanly shaven chin.

"The only connection between this deal and Atlantic City is the doctor's gambling debts," he said. "As far as your authorities are concerned, there's no way they can connect us to the Atlantic City people. And second, you're wrong. They *are* our friends, as long as we play straight with them."

"What about that dead doctor's wife you were so chummy with?" said Lena, raising her voice. "Hell, she didn't even wait two months before marrying the other partner. Talk about a smell! That stinks to high heaven. Then you got the daughter—you get a dysfunctional family and anything goes."

"If it turns out to be a problem, I can fix it," said Carlos.

"That's not all that would need fixing. There's the other partner, the one so anxious to sell. As you pointed out, he's up to his neck in gambling debts, and I understand he has been enjoying his own merchandise."

Carlos stared blankly at the ceiling.

"No matter how clean you say your hands are, dear brother," Lena continued, "you have connections to all those people. If any of them get nailed for killing the doctor, you can bet your ass that they're not going out without dragging other people, like you and me, right down with them. I don't intend to wait around and risk being thrown under the bus—or, for that matter, put on the other side of the grass!"

"Okay, big sister, I'm sick of arguing with you," said Carlos. "Just tell me what you want me to do."

Lena didn't hesitate.

"We are going to get out of that damn town," she said.

Not long after their mansion spat, the twins found a buyer. The Commonwealth of Massachusetts made it easy by unwittingly providing the prospect list. All actions of the medical board are considered public record and are available online. It took Lena less than five minutes to compile a list of doctors reprimanded for writing prescriptions for controlled substances outside of their usual course of professional practice. The twins struck a deal with the fifth doctor on Lena's list.

The next step was to make it difficult for anyone to ask questions. From experience, Lena had learned that cops are like everyone else. They go for low-hanging fruit. Cold case files are full of crimes that would have necessitated travel to investigate. Long distance travel requires approval of travel vouchers. The last thing a cop wants to do is deal with an arrogant bean counter.

Lena arranged to move the surviving doctor and his new wife (the widow of his former partner) to Nashville. It was an offer the doctor couldn't turn down—a half million moving bonus and a guaranteed minimum annual income of three million dollars. All he had to do was open and supervise nine new clinics in small rural cities in Middle Tennessee.

Guaranteeing his salary was easy. Lena always had a termination clause for any employment contract. An employee could only collect if he was alive. In the doctor's case, if he weren't up to the job or if Massachusetts should come calling, he would simply have a deadly car wreck on some curvy country road.

There was only one person Lena considered indispensable. Carlos. And it wasn't because of his business savvy or muscle. Even though she and Carlos had shared a womb for nine months, it was not loyalty or love for her brother that made him irreplaceable. It was because Lena was sick, and Carlos, a perfect match for her blood, was her only hope.

Chapter 5

Sammie Miller

Sammie Miller was with her boyfriend, Billy, in his pickup. The teenagers' families lived in Franklin, Tennessee, a wealthy suburb of Nashville. Billy was on a mission. He had driven to Coffee County about sixty miles south of Franklin. He had an idea, a rather stupid idea, about how he and Sammie could get money to buy more Percocet. They could steal storm drains.

Not long before, Sammie had been a perfect student with straight A's. Then something happened. She was a stunning seventeen-year-old who, if she had chosen differently, could have made a lot of money as a model, a centerfold, some perfect face in a clothing catalog. Instead, she began dating Billy Underwood. Out of boredom, both started playing around with narcotics. Not street drugs like heroin. That wouldn't have been cool. What was cool was getting high on illegally acquired *legal* pain medications—opioids. The drug enforcement authorities called it drug diversion—legally prescribed pain medication (controlled substances) diverted illegally for recreational purposes. The preferred happy pills for Sammie and her friends were Percs, a combination of Oxycodone and acetaminophen. While Oxycodone sparks the addiction, the acetaminophen eventually kills the user, provided he or she doesn't overdose first.

Billy stole his first pills from his parents. Then, for a while, before Sammie's stepfather (a doctor) left, the two had an unlimited supply. Percs were everywhere in her house—like candy—and no one was keeping track. When her stepfather left, so did the pills. By then, the two young people were hooked and hooked bad. Their appetite for Percs couldn't be satisfied with the few pilfered pills that Billy was still able to get from his parents. They tried stealing from some elderly people's homes in their Franklin neighborhood, taking whatever they could find in medicine cabinets. Sammie liked the adrenalin rush she got from the thefts. After they broke into a random house while the couple was away on some errand, she and Billy had sex for the first time. It hurt badly. But she kept working at it with Billy and soon she began to enjoy it. Billy was no great lover. He was selfish, distracted, and then it was all over. She knew there should be more to it, and she thought that someday she might try it with someone else.

What they got from medicine cabinets wasn't always Percocet. Most of the time, they weren't sure what they were taking. Life was a roller coaster of highs and lows, pain and relief, and a constant pursuit of the next high.

They stopped thinking about stealing pills and started thinking about where to get the money to buy them. As dopers go, Sammie and Billy were amateurs. To them, Percs were anything containing Oxy. The real Percocet brand is a low-dosage tablet, 2.5, 5, 7.5, and 10 milligram pills. You had to eat Percocet by the handful to get high. It didn't take long before the two preferred generics, some as high as 60 milligrams per tablet. They thought in terms of milligrams and pill colors. Roxidone 15 milligram greens and 30 milligram blues were the most readily available at about fifteen dollars and thirty dollars a pill. Some people had started crushing the pills to get high quicker. Sammie and Billy still swallowed their prize whole. Using a needle and shooting up was down the road, but they were speeding in that direction.

Once a user becomes part of the "happy pill" community, buying becomes easy—provided you have the money. Drugs consume everything. Other plans or pursuits quickly fall away. Junkies talk exclusively about the drug—where to get it and how to get the money to buy the next stash. Druggies are buying, sharing, selling, or hunting for money. If you're flush, you share with your closest friends. If you're crashing, you beg those same friends for some of their stash. Each person in the drug community wants everyone in the community to be high—flush with drugs. A druggie's biggest fear is drying out with no one to turn to for a share of their stash. If everyone is flush, there is always a source. If I share with you, the thinking goes, then you'll share with me.

Where to score becomes the paramount question, the one inquiry that eclipses everything else. There are wholesalers in almost all neighborhoods, but they are beyond the reach of most addicts. Wholesalers are businesspeople who get involved for profit—big profit. They are usually clean themselves and very selective about who they sell to. The problem is that you can't trust a druggie customer, so wholesalers usually get busted after a few years. For users like Sammie and Billy, the supply is unstable. They get their drugs wherever they can find them, and they take dangerous risks to score. Stealing iron drainage pipes can suddenly seem reasonable.

Most addicts with money buy from other addicts—*sources*—who sell to fund their own habits. Those sources get their supply through a variety of means: from wholesalers, through a cohort in the medical or pharmaceutical field, from pill mills (pain clinics that write prescriptions for cash), by doctor shopping, over the Internet, or from international mules such as flight attendants and pilots who make over-the-counter purchases in Southeast Asia or black-market purchases of Chinese pharmaceuticals while outside the United States. If addicts are desperate enough, they will steal and rob. Some will even kill.

For an addict without money, there is another source—people who barter drugs for sex. The clients are almost all men. Some are looking for boys, but most are using drugs to get young girls to perform. Finally, some are human traffickers looking to shanghai their victims into a short life as a prostitute or sex slave. What happens after that doesn't matter.

— ƒ —

Billy was driving through the streets of Coffee County neighborhoods. The signs of new home construction were everywhere—people moving south of Nashville and Murfreesboro for lower home prices.

He and Sammie peered obsessively from the windows, searching for storm drains.

Suddenly Sammie said, "Goddammit, Billy, I don't want to do this anymore. I almost broke my thumb on that last one! Don't we have enough already?"

Sweat ran into Billy's eyes. He tried to wipe it away as he said, "Look, Sammie, we wouldn't have to screw with these damn storm drains if you had just slept with that guy last night. That was five hundred bucks. You just walked away. Man, we could have gotten fifteen or twenty blues—I'm talking thirty milligrams a shot. It wouldn't have been a big deal for you. I bet the guy would have shot his rocks off just watching you take off your clothes. Even if he held it together, he probably wouldn't have lasted five minutes."

Sammie cringed.

"You don't know that, Billy!" she shouted. "The guy could have been a pervert. I could have gotten AIDS or something."

"Come on. It's not like you're a virgin. You could have made him use a rubber. I wouldn't have let him hurt you or anything."

"Goddammit, Billy, I'm not a whore."

Billy's shakes were getting worse. He was hyper from the itching. "Oh, goddammit! Shit! Son of a bitch!" he sputtered. Billy pounded on the steering wheel until the cramp went away.

They had already loaded four of the heavy iron grates into the back of Billy's truck. Billy's sweat was dripping now—the itching was so bad he couldn't sit still. He gritted his teeth as he said, "Can you believe it, Sammie? The county paid 250 bucks to purchase each of those things. It's like stealing candy from a baby. I mean, nobody stands guard over a friggin' drain. A thousand dollars' worth of drains in half an hour isn't bad. If we can just get eight more—that's three thousand dollars and a lot of Blues."

The storm drains were Billy's plan for quick cash. He had worked for the county for two weeks before they fired him for not showing up. He heard the foreman talking about the storm drains. Sammie felt that there was something wrong with the plan but wasn't thinking clearly enough to figure it out.

"Billy, who are we going to sell these drains to?"

Billy was sweating profusely now. Sammie was beginning to feel a pit in her stomach. It was hot. Like Billy, sweat was dripping down her cheeks. The air conditioning in the truck didn't work, but she also felt clammy and cold. What she and Billy needed, and needed now, were their happy pills, Percs. Suddenly she thought doing it with that guy didn't sound that bad. She had taken her last two yellow Percocets, 10 milligrams each, just as Billy pulled up in his truck to pick her up. What she really wanted were Blues or three or four Greens, but at least the Yellows had kept her from crashing hard. They needed to make a buy soon—something that would hang for a while.

"I looked it up on the net," said Billy. "There's a place in Shelbyville. They buy scrap metal, and I don't think they ask questions. What is it to them where it comes from anyway?"

"Shit, that's an hour drive from here, Billy. I can't wait that long. We'll both be puking our guts out by the time we get back home and find someone selling."

"No, no," Billy argued. "I know this place in Shelbyville. It's a pain clinic. The doctor moved here from Florida."

Billy doubled over, holding his stomach.

"Oh, God, the cramps! So help me, Sammie, if you got a hidden stash, I need them now! Goddammit. Give it to me, now!"

"I don't have any, Billy," cried Sammie. "I'm on empty. Let's go sell what we have now—no more looking for other drains."

"If I find out you've been holding out on me, *so help me God*, I'll rip you a new one! Oh, God! Sam, hold the steering wheel, will you? I'm going to puke!"

Sammie slid across the seat of the truck, grasping the steering wheel while stretching for the brake pedal. She steered toward the shoulder of the road as Billy opened the driver-side door of the truck, leaned out, and threw up.

What neither Sammie nor Billy realized was that a Coffee County sheriff's car had been following their truck for the last mile and a half. As the truck rolled to a stop on the side of the road, two quick pulses of the car's siren told the teens that they were in serious shit.

Chapter 6

Women's Health Club

Lately people have started to attach my name to the place, as in: "Mark Rollins's Club." Granted, I own the place, but I still prefer for people to use its initials, WHC. I had been away from the club for almost a month while I resolved the remaining issues related to the claret murders matter. My daughter, Margaret Rollins Scott, who everyone calls "Meg," keeps it running day to day. Nevertheless, our wealthy female clients expect to see my face around the place from time to time. That's part of its *shtick,* or so the PR people keep telling me. Frankly, I like being there.

As mentioned before, the official name of the WHC is the Women's Health Club. As far as the public is concerned, it is an exclusive fitness facility for the wealthy and elite women of the greater Nashville, Tennessee, area. What most people don't know is that the WHC is also my "bat cave"—the cover for an extraordinary high-tech center and a group of technology geeks I call my "brain trust."

― ✘ ―

It was a beautiful, early summer day as my driver Tony and I reached Brentwood. The trees in town were finally leafed out. Winter was now well behind us. One lane of Franklin Road was closed to cars. Brentwood is a favorite place for bike races and cause-related runs. Today's runners were wearing orange ribbons.

The 6:15 a.m. boot camp had wrapped up at WHC, and participants were pulling out of the parking lot as I arrived at the Maryland Way location. I had a feeling of déjà vu. The first time I met the talented Mariko Lee, she was the instructor of the camp. She was as tough on the boot camp participants as a Marine drill sergeant. Back then she looked like a teenage boy—short hair, camping boots, cargo shorts, and barely over five feet tall. I discovered rather quickly that she was an ex-Marine MP with a certified Black Belt in Tae Kwon Do. She was also licensed to carry, and she did. Mariko was a biker who liked leather, but she leaned toward the exotic when it came to her appearance and the outfits she wore. She wasn't just muscle. It turned out that she was a trust fund baby with a postgraduate degree from Vanderbilt's Owen School of Business. It wasn't long before I was depending on her—first as a driver, then as a bodyguard, and now as WHC's vice president of security. I looked forward to seeing her again and getting a rundown on any new security issues.

The early morning boot camp continues to be popular. I have always been surprised by how many of our club members are willing to show up early in the morning for an hour and a half of intense aerobics. But then, they tend to be the wives or daughters of Nashville's rich and famous—willing to sacrifice a lot for a perfect bikini-and-evening-dress body. They work hard and I have to say, for the most part, they have achieved their objective.

While Tony parked the car, I entered the building through the employee's rear door. For security purposes, entrance to the building is limited to members and employees. Members can come through the main entrance using a pass card alongside a manually-entered key code. All other entrances are employees-only and require a retinal scan. As far as the members are concerned, the need for security is to protect them from the growing trend of kidnapping for ransom. Our members wear a lot of bling when working out. While kidnapping the rich is not usually a North American problem, our jet-set members think internationally—and it *is* a problem in many countries. Of course, it's the clandestine nature of the WHC that really necessitates the unusual security.

I headed for my office near the front reception area. Shannon, our receptionist, aware of my arrival because it was caught on camera, was waiting for me.

"Welcome back, Mr. Rollins," she said. "Everyone has been asking about you."

"Thanks, Shannon," I said, noticing an orange band on her wrist just like on the runners around town. "The last time I saw you wearing orange it was for feral cats. So, what's it this time?"

"That was so long ago, Mr. Rollins," she said. "This is much more important."

Shannon's enthusiasm bubbled over each time she supported a new cause. And she always seemed to have one.

"Orange is the color for Feeding America!" she said enthusiastically. "Did you know that 17 percent of people in Tennessee suffer from *food insecurity?*"

"Food insecurity? What happened to hunger, Shannon?"

"Well, not everyone suffers from hunger all the time now that we have so many government programs," she said. "But even with the programs, sometimes people don't have enough to eat. That is food insecurity—not always having enough to eat. That is awful! Thankfully, now Feed America is going to eliminate food insecurity."

"But wait a minute, Shannon," I said. "What about obesity? Can you be overweight and still be insecure that you didn't get enough to eat?"

"Mr. Rollins, are you making fun of me again?"

"I'm sorry, Shannon," I said. "I think it's nice that you care about people and animals. Stop by my office later and I'll have a check for you. But, first I want to get an update from Meg on the club."

"Oh, thank you! I knew you would. We can always count on you, Mr. Rollins."

I took the elevator up to Meg's second-floor office. I was still using a cane so I avoided the stairs. Tony took the stairs two at time, joining me as I entered Meg's office.

"So, Meg, what's working and what isn't?" I asked.

"Hi, Pop and Tony!" she said with a smile. "Glad to see you back in the shop, Dad."

"Seriously, Meg. Make me feel needed. What's going on?"

"Well, nothing stays the same when it comes to the fitness scene except the fact that the customers are almost all blondes."

From Meg's desk, she could view any of the seven workout rooms, A through G, on a large monitor mounted on the wall opposite her desk.

As she switched to room E, she said, "For example, note all the blondes with drumsticks. They are weighted Ripstix. Classes fuse Pilates, isometric movements, and plyometrics. Believe it or not, you can burn up to nine hundred calories in less than an hour while sculpting muscles with simulated drumming to rhythmic music. The new workout is called *Pound*, invented by two former drummers. Let me show you another new routine. This is room A."

Meg stopped talking and looked at Tony and me, waiting excitedly for our reaction.

After a few seconds, Tony said, "That's quite a show."

I said, "Right! We could start a new revenue stream by charging admission."

"I thought that would be your reaction to our new pole dancing workout," said Meg. "But I tried it, and I tell you it has the sweat pouring out of you in just a few minutes. It's a very effective workout. Our ladies are crazy about the opportunity to flaunt their womanly curves while getting healthier at the same time."

"Unfortunately for me," I said, "it looks like you have it all under control. I don't feel very needed. What about Mariko? Where is she today?"

"She's taking care of a little security problem."

"Oh?"

"It seems that one of our customers has a stalker," said Meg. "The club member thinks he is cute. However, he hangs around the club's parking areas and snaps photos of other customers as they are leaving. Some of them don't agree with the notion that he's cute and innocent. They think he's creepy."

"How is Mariko handling it?"

"Turns out he is nineteen. Mariko tracked down his mother. She is only forty-two. In decent shape. Mariko is giving her a six-month complimentary membership to the Women's Health Club. In fact, she's bringing her to the club today for an orientation tour. Mariko figures that once the mother shows up, the boy will split. If he doesn't, his mother is likely to spot him and rein him in."

"Sounds like a smart plan to me," I said.

"I thought so too."

"Listen, we're having a case wind-down lunch at Sperry's today," I said. "You are welcome to join us. I know we leave you high and dry to run the place on your own while Tony, Mariko, and I are off on our little adventures, but you are as much a part of the problem-solving team as anyone. Bryan's people will be there, as will Sam Littleton."

Meg scrunched her eyes, trying to place the name to a face.

"You remember Sam," I continued. "He's the head guy in the FBI office and is the chair of the joint task force on terrorists' active in the region."

"Uh, yeah!" said Meg. "Thanks, Dad. I didn't know Sperry's opened for lunch."

"They don't," I said. "At least they don't for everyone. But every now and then, I get them to open for me and a few friends."

"Okay, Dad. I'll join you if I can. In case I get tied up, please don't wait on me though."

— ʃ —

It was 2:30 in the afternoon before our little band of misfits finished lunch—one of our ritual end-of-case closure sessions held as usual at Sperry's in Belle Meade. We called the recently wrapped case *The Claret Murders*. We celebrated, if you can call it that, with an extraordinary red Bordeaux, or as the English would say, a "claret." It may well have been the last 1947 magnum of *Chateau Cheval Blanc* on earth. The claret was the only bottle I could recover from the Taylor mansion after a devastating Nashville flood. As we poured the last round of that otherworldly wine, a vintage that connoisseur and author Mike Steinberger called "a claret from another planet," my iPhone signaled a new text message. I looked down at the screen: *Mr. Rollins, I have a serious problem and need your help. Please call ASAP—it's critically important!*

I'm afraid I had more than my share of wine, so I was happy to slide into the back seat of Black Beauty and let Tony do the driving as we headed back to the WH Club. I needed to decide what to do about the message I had just received.

Black Beauty was the nickname my team of technical wizards gave my modified Lexus, GS 350. From within Black Beauty, I had full Internet access and secure communications. Its sides were armored, as was the glass, and my team retrofitted some rather aggressive defense capabilities that probably break more than a few laws. I made it a point not to ask.

My driver, Tony Caruso, is an ex-submariner with the characteristic small frame. People tend to underestimate him—to his advantage. Tony is a good man to have around when trouble hits. He is an expert evasive driver and a decorated marksman, a sharpshooter. I've seen him blow out the center of a target from a standing position—rapid firing a full magazine from his Glock. Like me he's licensed to carry, but for defensive purposes he prefers a tactical baton over a handgun. The problem with a handgun is the danger a stray bullet poses to an innocent bystander. You don't have that problem with a wand. You can take out a bad guy's knee or break his wrist with a single blow.

The text message I received at Sperry's was a surprise, but not because it was a request for help. I've gotten used to those. My fitness club plays host to around five hundred of Nashville's elite women. Somehow, I seem to have become a father figure or big brother for many of them. What surprised me was the name, Glenda Adams. Glenda and my son, Dan, had been friends all the way through high school. She and Dan went to a few dances and parties together when they didn't have other dates, but I don't believe there was ever any love interest between them. They double-dated. She had boyfriends and Dan had girlfriends. Dan and Glenda were just good buddies. You don't see that much—a boy and girl in their teens who are just friends. She was a regular around the Rollins's compound. What I remembered most about her was her laugh. She and Dan laughed a lot when they were together. Those were happy years.

After high school, Dan went one way and she went another. She went off to a Boston university with dreams of becoming a doctor. We lost contact with her, until now— *Please call ASAP—it's critically important!* The text was short and to the point—too short and too direct. The Glenda I remembered would have sounded friendlier. We Southerners always begin any message or conversation with a few niceties no matter how desperate or solemn the situation. From Glenda, I would expect something like, *Hello, Mr. Rollins, how are you and your family?* Then she might have gotten around to asking for help. There were no niceties in her text message. Of course, text messages don't really lend themselves to a conversational style. They tend to fall on the "Just the facts, ma'am" side of things. Still, the short message coming from the person I had known heightened my concern for her.

Any other time, I would have hung around Sperry's for coffee and sharing some war stories about our adventures, but finding out what was up with Glenda was far more important.

The car's communication system automatically syncs with traffic to and from my iPhone, so it was easy to place a call to the source of the message. I clicked on the text appearing on the car's display and selected the voice call option.

The phone had not even finished its first ring when she answered.

"Hello?"

"Glenda, it's Mark, Mark Rollins."

"Thank God," she said. "I've been going out of my mind."

Chapter 7

Sammie's Arrest

She sounded both relieved and exasperated.
"What's wrong, Glenda?" I asked.
"It's my daughter," she said, almost breathless. "She's been arrested. She's at a jail in Manchester. Mark, I'm sick, very sick—cancer. We just buried my parents—a car wreck. My husband has disappeared. Now this! I didn't have anyone to turn to. That's why I called to ask you for help. Please, Mark—please. I'm scared I might die and my daughter won't have anybody."

My stomach knotted. The desperation and sheer panic in her voice instantly dissolved the memory of a young, vivacious Glenda. This was a new image. One I didn't like—a sick, frightened, broken woman, begging for help. I knew right then, no matter what, that I was going to try to save her. I wanted the old image back, and I was going to do whatever I had to do to make that happen.

"Glenda, whatever it is, we'll fix it," I said. "We'll put things right and you are not going to die. I will not let you. Now first, tell me everything you know about your daughter."

I could hear her sigh deeply into the receiver.

"Oh, God, thank you," she said. "You have no idea how helpless I feel. You were my only hope. Honest, Mr. Rollins, I don't know what I would have done if you hadn't called me back. I . . . I . . . I'm sorry."

The tears she had been choking back broke through. They were deep, slow sobs—she didn't have to tell me. I knew they were a release from the feeling of hopelessness. I had given her a shoulder to cry on—one that I think she knew she could rely on to stay with her throughout the ordeals ahead. It wasn't just about the daughter. I was going to save her, and it was going to cost me. I was going to have to absorb some of the emotional black cloud that was weighing so heavily on this person. Whatever burden time and misfortune had inflicted on her, she was still that young friend of Dan's—the one who spent so much time with us years ago. The one we had opened our home and our hearts to.

When the crying finally stopped, she managed to say, "I don't know much, Mr. Rollins."

There was a long silence.

"Take your time, Glenda," I said.

"Sammie, that's what we call my daughter, phoned me from the jail. She was so upset and I didn't get a lot out of her. Sammie was with her boyfriend. His name is Underwood—Billy Underwood."

Glenda's voice was breaking up again. I could tell she was trying hard to keep from crying.

"Sammie said something about storm drains," she continued. "Please, Mr. Rollins, can you do something? I can't think straight. The chemo has made me so sick—I can't drive."

"What is Sammie's real name?"

"What? Oh, it's Samantha Miller," she said. "I've gone back to my maiden name—Adams. I had Sammie with my first husband, Raymond Miller. He died."

"Don't hang up, Glenda," I said. "I'm going to put you on hold for a few minutes."

"Okay."

Tony had been listening to my side of the conversation so he knew something was afoot.

"Tony, we have a change of plans. We need to go to Manchester—the Manchester jail."

"Sure thing, Mr. R," said Tony. "A problem of some kind?"

"Yes, the daughter of an old friend is currently a guest of the Coffee County sheriff."

"That's not good," he said. "I would put our ETA ninety minutes from now. I can try to make it in sixty or less, if you want."

"I want to go to the jail not be put in it!" I said. "Get us there as quickly as you can and still keep us legal."

Before going back to Glenda, I selected another phone line and called Bryan, the head of the WHC brain trust.

"Yo, Chief, what can I do for you?"

"Bryan, I don't have time to brief you now, but I need you to clear your desk and review the status of your team members. When I call you back in a few, I'll have some top priority issues. You'll need to know staff availability. Okay?"

"I'm on it, Chief."

Bryan didn't expect me to say anything else. I disconnected. The icon for the call on hold was flashing on the display in front of me. The wireless keyboard and mouse were on a fold-down shelf like an airplane's tray table. Before clicking on the icon to return to Glenda's call, I used the keyboard to make a few notes—things I wanted to be sure to ask her. Then I clicked.

Chapter 8

Glenda Adams

After reconnecting to Glenda's phone, I heard sobs.
"Glenda, I'm back."
"Thank goodness," she said. "I was afraid we'd been disconnected." She started to cry again. "I don't know what to do."

"Glenda, it's going to be all right," I said. "I'll take care of it. Please don't worry. But you have to tell me everything you know about your daughter's arrest and what you think might have led up to it."

"I've been so sick and Sammie has been fending for herself."

"Start at the beginning," I said. "Tell me about when you went to college, got married; about Sammie, your first husband, your second marriage, when you got sick, etc. We have about an hour—tell me your story."

I heard her take a deep breath. I gave her a little time to collect her thoughts. Turns out Glenda left Franklin to go to college in 1988. She had wanted to go to Harvard but didn't make the cut. She *did*, however, get into Northeastern University where she majored in pre-med and graduated in 1993. After that she started medical school, this time at Harvard, but she never finished.

"I got through three years and then Sammie intervened in 1996," she said.

Sammie's father, I soon learned, was Raymond Miller, an MD in anesthesiology. He and Glenda were married as soon as she discovered she was pregnant. The plan was that she would go back to med school once Sammie was old enough for daycare, but that never worked out.

"Ray and another anesthesiologist, Yusuf Arian, opened a pain intervention clinic in the Quincy area of Boston," she said. "We were happy, at first. Sammie was a great baby. She got older, did well in school, and had lots and lots of friends. Then everything started to change."

"When was that, Glenda?" I asked.

"I can't put my finger on it exactly, but it started to boil to the surface when Sammie was a teenager, around 2009," she said. "The clinic had been doing so well there was never any need for me to go back to med school. But Ray started to change. Then there was a lawsuit. A patient died during an operation. Ray was accused of being impaired."

I interrupted. "Drugs?"

"It was alcohol. It was an early morning operation, and we had been at a party the night before. Anyway, things were never the same after that."

Glenda explained how her husband didn't like being a doctor anymore, how he started drinking heavily. Ray gained a lot of weight, she said, and he just stopped caring about how he looked or dressed. There were many nights when he didn't come home. Glenda insisted it wasn't an affair—that he just stayed at the clinic.

"He even had a bed there," she said sounding slightly embarrassed. "I told him he didn't care about how he looked anymore, but it was more than that. Maybe he was depressed. He just stopped caring about Sammie and me. Then he got mean. He was nasty to people. Our friends stopped calling us or inviting us to things."

Glenda took a deep breath, as if preparing for the next stage of the story.

"When Ray didn't come home and we needed something, his partner, Yusuf Arian, was always ready to help. I couldn't have made it through the last few years without Yusuf's help," she continued.

Glenda described how Yusuf decided he wanted to sell the clinic to some investment group and how such hand-offs were becoming a trend. She said doctors were becoming employees, working for hospitals and clinics owned by corporations or entrepreneurial businesspersons.

"It would have meant a lot of money and Ray would still get a salary—a big salary," she said.

I already knew of the trend, which was understandable considering the increase in regulation and the billing complications—the business side had become too complex.

"Doctors trying to operate on their own can't keep up," I said.

"Yes, that's right," said Glenda. "That's why Yusuf pushed the idea so hard. Ray wouldn't agree. I was on

Yusuf's side. I wasn't feeling right. I really wanted to move back to Nashville. I begged Ray to sell."

Glenda had since realized that her desire for the sale probably made Ray more opposed to the idea. Yusuf and Ray had a big falling out over the issue. The two stopped talking to each other. She was in the middle because she thought Yusuf was right.

"What happened next?" I asked.

"Then Ray died," said Glenda. "Yusuf found him. It was the middle of the day. Ray had patients in the waiting room but hadn't come out of the bedroom he kept at his office so the nurse finally went to Yusuf about it. Yusuf went to check on him. That's when he found him. Ray was still in the bed, the one he kept at the clinic."

I imagined the shock, the first phone call. I imagined Sammie suddenly without a dad.

"Under the terms of their partners' agreement," she continued, "upon the death of one of the partners, ownership goes to the surviving partner. That left me out in the cold."

Glenda explained how Yusuf then owned the clinic outright and how he went ahead with the sale to the investment group that had been trying to buy them. Yusuf got a ten-year employment contract with the new owners and, although he didn't have to, he got the buyer to agree to make monthly payments to Glenda for seven years.

"Five months after Ray's death," said Glenda, "Yusuf and I were married."

"Were you and Yusuf having an affair before your husband's death?" I asked.

"Oh, God, no!" she said without hesitation. "It wasn't like that. Not at all. He had been so helpful. We just kind of gravitated toward each other after Ray was gone."

"Sorry," I said. "I had to ask. What about the cause of death?"

"They said his heart just stopped. There were some hints of drugs. No one wanted to push it—you know the *white lab-coat curtain* came down. Doctors, like cops, protect each other."

"I'll try to find out more of the details about his death later," I said. "For now, let's get back to your story."

Glenda said that shortly after she and Yusuf were married, they moved to Franklin. She wanted to be close to her parents.

"We waited until Sammie had finished the ninth grade," she said. "After the move, she enrolled in Franklin High School."

According to Glenda, what really made the move possible was the opportunity for Yusuf. The new owners of the clinic also owned similar operations in Florida. They were expanding into other states. Yusuf was to open and oversee the operation of several clinics in small communities in Middle Tennessee.

I nodded to myself. I had heard about similar expansions.

"That was when things really started to go bad," said Glenda. "Ray's death was hard enough, but right after the move, both my parents were killed in a terrible car wreck. They were on Hillsboro Road, turning onto Spencer Creek Road. They were hit from behind, pushed into the oncoming traffic, and T-boned by a dump truck."

Her story just kept getting worse. After she lost her parents, Glenda underwent exploratory surgery and woke up with an ostomy and stage IV colon cancer. She didn't think Yusuf could take it. He had gotten in trouble gambling once before, she said. He started doing it again. He would go to Tunica or Atlantic City on weekends. He made withdrawals from her account at UBS—money she and Ray had invested for the future.

"At first, I thought maybe he was having an affair or maybe it was a midlife crisis," she said. "I'm sure now it was his way of escaping. He was not a drinker like Ray, but there were always a lot of pills around. Last weekend, he got in his car and hasn't come back. I don't know where he is."

I interrupted again. "His name suggests he was of Middle Eastern descent?"

"His parents were Syrian, I think," she said. "He was born in the United States."

"What about his parents? Have they heard from him?"

"They're dead. Yusuf doesn't have any family left that I know of."

"Have you filed a missing person report?" I asked.

"No, I guess I just kept thinking he would show up. Now, I don't know."

"What about his clothes, money, car, cell phone?"

"I tried calling," she said. "I just get his voice message."

Glenda said Yusuf always kept a suitcase in his car because he would have to drive to the clinics he was to manage. As for money, she was still receiving her monthly payments from the investment group. He had his own account.

"Mine isn't a joint account either," she said. "Nor were my investments at UBS. Unfortunately, he knew my passwords. I changed those when I realized he was withdrawing my money. We had a very bad fight about that. That's another reason I thought he left."

"How about Sammie? How did she feel about his leaving?"

"To be honest, it was almost like she didn't notice," she said. "I'm worried now—all those pills that Yusuf left around the house. What if she got into those? I'm not sure I can handle that. My Sammie on drugs."

Glenda began sobbing again.

"Glenda, all of us did stupid things when we were young. We'll get it straightened out."

"God, I hope so. I hope so, Mark."

"Do you have a list of the clinics?"

"No. I know that's bad, but it was Yusuf's business," she said. "With everything else going on, I wasn't paying attention to him or Sammie. Oh my—that's so bad after hearing me say it out loud. I feel like this is my fault."

"You said 'everything else going on.' What did you mean by that?"

"I mean the cancer," she said. "I found out just after we moved. I was so stupid not to have had the tests doctors recommended. They all sounded so horrible. I ignored the doctors' advice and now I'm paying for it big time. I'm afraid the outlook isn't very good, Mark."

"We'll talk about that later. Glenda, I've been where you are."

I told her of some people getting remarkable results in treatments for colon cancer. They saved my life; they could save hers too.

"When we get this immediate problem with Sammie taken care of, I want to arrange to have you see them," I said. "Has Sammie been in trouble before?"

"No. *Never!*"

"Okay, we're getting close to Manchester, so I'm going to let you go for now. I have a few things I want to check on before I talk to the sheriff."

"Okay, but call me as soon as you see my daughter."

"I will."

I disconnected. Took a long drink of water. The air conditioning in the car was set on sixty-eight degrees—freezing by my wife's standards, but I was sweating. I put down the bottle of water and called Bryan.

Chapter 9

Bryan Gray

As usual, Bryan popped online before the end of the first ringtone.

"Okay, I'm ready for you, Chief," he said in a quick cadence. "What's up?"

Bryan and I have worked together for more than twenty years. Long ago we gave up chit chat or phone niceties like *hello* and *goodbye*. Our calls are usually succinct and always limited to business.

"I need to know who's who at the Manchester jail and in the Coffee County sheriff's department," I said. "Do any of the players owe us favors? Also, check to see what you have on two teenagers: one Samantha Miller, aka Sammie or Sammie Miller, and a boyfriend known as Billy Underwood—probably William. Also, see what you can get quickly on the girl's mother, maiden name Glenda Adams. Include medical in your probe."

"Chief, you need to give me at least one specific on the mother as a starting point for my searches—a location, employer, anything you've got."

"You can access my system in the Lexus, right?"

"Sure."

"Okay," I said. "The last call on my cell line one is the mother. You can use it to get her current address. Also, she went to high school with my son. Went to Boston for college at Northeastern University. Check medical colleges in the area too. She stayed in the area until recently returning to the current local address that you can get from the phone number."

"Okay, that's enough to get me started," he said. "When do you want this, Chief?"

"I'm in route to Manchester. I need something before I arrive."

"Okay. I'll give you what I can come up with in an hour. I'll divide it up and get the entire team working on it. But it's going to be a pretty limited dump."

"I need you to break rules if need be," I said. "I need answers to some questions by the time I get to Manchester. Here's the scoop."

Bryan was all ears. I explained the entire sordid story in as few words as possible.

"Find out the cancer status, and get the scoop on husband number one, now dead, and husband number two, now missing. You got that, Bryan?"

"Roger, Chief!"

Typical of Bryan, he was off the line and going to work on my checklist. He had a lot of resources to work with. The WHC has more electronics than most CIA satellite operation centers. Obviously, there is no apparent justification for the technology resources at the club. Initially, it was just a luxury I could afford to continue even though I was no longer engaged commercially in the tech industry. Today, however, this low visibility operation inside of the Women's Health Club is embarrassingly profitable due to its off-the-record role with various government agencies. As I mentioned, the WHC doesn't have to play by the same rules; thus, in cyberspace, Bryan and his team can do things and go places that official arms of our government cannot. For that, the WHC's clandestine team gets paid the big bucks.

It also means that there isn't much that can escape the eyes and ears of my team. When I need answers, Bryan and his crew have always delivered, every time.

Chapter 10

Tom Lewis

Coffee County deputy Tom Lewis was a thirty-seven-year-old low life. Never finished high school. The only decent thing he ever did was to marry his fourteen-year-old girlfriend after getting her pregnant. There was nothing decent about how he treated her after the marriage, though. She ran away after three years and took the child with her. She hasn't been heard from since.

Tom—a tall, thin, pale man with deep set eyes and a perpetual five o'clock shadow—lived in an unkempt mobile home on a piece of land owned by his parents. The trailer faced Old Cemetery Road and, by its mere presence, lowered the adjacent property values. If his place had been inside Manchester's city limits, it would have been condemned. But it wasn't. Old Cemetery Road was a poorly kept, one-lane country road. The twenty-five feet between his front door and the road was filled with junk and trash—empty whisky bottles, old tires, a refrigerator that stopped working years ago, and rusty barrels full of garbage waiting to be burned. Anything that did not have a place elsewhere or stopped working was parked there, either because Tom thought he might have a use for it someday or because he was too lazy to care. There was an old kitchen table with mismatched chairs under one of the trees between the trailer and the road where he used to hold council with his drinking buddies.

Tom did little more than sleep and dress in the trailer. He took showers under a hose connected to a water pipe by the front door. There was no working bathroom in the trailer. When he had to go, he went behind the trailer. Somehow, he had managed to get on the sheriff's staff working at the jail, a job his father probably got for him. It didn't pay much, but then he didn't do much. He also moonlighted as security at the new pain clinic, and worked a side-scam that supplied most of his money. About the only clothes he owned were his uniforms, which always looked like he had slept in them. He usually had. The trailer had electricity, a TV, and a satellite dish. When Tom wasn't working at the jail or the clinic, he spent his time and his money drinking, watching porn on his TV, or hunting for someone he could buy sex from.

When one of the deputies brought Sammie and her boyfriend into the jail, Tom Lewis couldn't stop looking at her. Normally, she would have been way out of his league. He knew that. The crap he heard she was hooked on made things different, however. That's why he called Rocco.

Rocco owned and ran the only Manchester whorehouse—more politely called a bordello. He was from "up north"—New Jersey and New York. By 2014, Rocco had been in business for twenty-three years and had never been arrested. His clientele included politicians, preachers, members of the sheriff's department, and teachers. Rocco, the transplanted Yankee, had become an accepted part of the little southern town—albeit its underbelly.

"Rocco, it's Tom Lewis over at the jail."

"Yo, man, what's up?"

"We've got a babe over here that you won't believe," Tom whispered. "I'm talking about some fine stuff."

"What's she in for?"

"Some dumb shit. She and her boyfriend were stealing storm drains."

"What the hell for?" asked Rocco.

"I told you it was dumb. From what I've heard, they thought they could sell the metal to buy some Oxy. That's why I called you."

"I'm not a grocery store, man," snapped Rocco. "I don't sell no dope!"

"No, no, no, that's not what I mean, Rocco. She's in a bad way. If you've got some Oxy, my guess is she would do just about anything you wanted for those pills. You know what I mean? I figure in our business you got some of the stuff around, but if you don't, I can sell you some. I do a little business on the side, you know. I'll tell you, Rocco, she isn't like those whores of yours. You can make a bundle off this little bombshell. She would put you in a different league—kick your image all the way uptown. Know what I mean?"

"Why are you suddenly being so nice to me?" asked Rocco. "What's in it for you?"

"I would just like to spend a little time with her myself," said Tom. "That's what. Jesus, just thinking about that gives me a hard-on."

"How do you suppose I'm going to get her out of your jail, man?"

"Right now, she hasn't been charged with anything," said Tom. "Her boyfriend was real gallant. Told them it was all him. She was just there for the ride. She didn't know what he was planning, and all the time she was trying to get him to stop. Sheriff wants her out of here. He's hoping that some tight ass 'responsible adult family member' will come get her."

"Right!" laughed Rocco. "You expect me to walk into your jail and tell the police I'm her daddy?"

"You're a funny man, Rocco. Of course not! Everybody knows you. You don't have to put one of your big New York feet inside the jail. I'm telling you, they don't have any restraints on her. You know Jimmy Lee, don't you?"

"Yeah, I know the lard-ass," said Rocco with a snort. "What about him?"

"He's my cousin, and he's on the front desk. I've already talked to him. So, if she just gets up and walks out, Jimmy isn't going to see that happen, and since she's not wearing restraints, nobody else is likely to try to stop her."

"I still don't understand," said Rocco. "What makes you think she would walk out and go anywhere with me? She don't know me from nothin'."

"You're not listening to me," hissed Tom. "She's a goddamn pill head! She's drying out, man! She is sicker than hell. Know what I mean? Look, you know I work at the clinic. Well, I get a couple of customers to give me some stuff for a place in line. So, if you need them, I can provide you with a few goddamn pills—just enough to stop the shakes and get her away from the toilet. You want to feed her an appetizer not a goddamn meal. Know what I mean? Keep her hungry for her little happy pills."

"Okay, okay, shithead," said Rocco. "I ain't exactly new to this game, you know. I give her a taste and promise her more. The doctor at the clinic is a customer of mine and, from time to time, he does a little bartering so I get my stuff. Now what? How do we make this work?"

"I tell her that I have someone—you—who will take her home and get her more pills," said Tom. "All she has to do is walk out and get in your car. Then you do whatever it is you do so that you own her. When you've got her all willing, I'll come around to collect my fee."

"What about family?" asked Rocco. "She doesn't sound like she's been living on the street or anything. I don't want to have some badass mommy or daddy coming after me 'cause I've got their baby girl. I don't need that, Tom."

"There's no daddy at home according to what I heard, and the mother doesn't seem interested enough to come collect her, at least not yet," said Tom confidently. "Man, you need to stop worrying. I'm telling you, Rocco, when you get a load of this little thing, you won't care who comes after you. You know how to handle people like that anyway. This is the nicest thing you are ever going to get your hands on. All it's going to cost you is a few freebies."

"I don't know," said Rocco.

"Shit, man—do I have to give you her statistics? This is no five-minute-job-in-the-back-seat-of-the-car whore. This is country club quality, man. You going to come get her or not?"

Chapter 11

Rocco Fantini

Rocco Fantini never knew exactly what his old man, Tonio Fantini, did back in Newark, New Jersey, but when Rocco was growing up, the family—Rocco's mother, two brothers and one sister—lived pretty good in their home in Roseville. Rocco's father had been a successful businessman in New Jersey's First Ward before Rocco was born. He owned a deli in the heart of an Italian neighborhood. In the 1950s, the city devastated the traditional ethnic Seventh Avenue area with a misguided urban renewal project. Tonio lost the deli. Displaced Italian families fled to other Newark neighborhoods—Broadway, Roseville, and the Ironbound.

Tonio was a handsome man, and he considered it his right to sample any willing nice-looking woman. After losing the deli, he never had a real job as far as Rocco knew. He had adopted Rocco's Uncle Gino's approach to living. Rocco remembered the uncle when he visited the family. Uncle Gino lived in Rome. He talked about the government's tax policies and explained how he and others in the Fantini family *just got by* doing some importing and other things to earn money that flew under the government's radar.

After closing the deli, that is exactly what Tonio Fantini did: he got by. He sold things that he laughingly said *fell off the truck*. Sometimes he would come home with cases of the same food item or a truckload of material—cloth for making suits or dresses. People would come to the house to buy things. Tonio also collected money for people. "Getting by" paid off so well that he started loaning his own money. As Rocco grew up, two things made Tonio different from other fathers. First, he always wore a white suit complete with vest and white wingtip shoes. Second, he never drove. He rode. He rode in a limo. His driver was Winston, a tall black man with a gold tooth. Winston had been a prizefighter, and Tonio hired him to help with the collection business.

When Rocco was starting high school, his sister Rose married a guy in the navy and moved to Millington near Memphis, Tennessee. A few years later, she wrote that they had moved to Manchester, Tennessee, where her husband, Alberto, had taken over the family's pizza joint. About that time, Rocco's mother passed away. There was no one home but Rocco and his dad.

The house did not stay womanless for long. Tonio invested in three Russian girls who moved into the house. He added prostitution to his *just getting by* sources of income. That's when Rocco discovered sex. The girls didn't speak English, but they were eager to learn. Rocco taught them English in exchange for bedroom privileges. That was more than okay with his dad. He bragged about his son's stamina—called him his *Italian Stallion*. What happened next was not okay with Rocco's old man. Rocco got the idea that he could pick up a little extra money by inviting some of his friends over when his dad wasn't around. That didn't go over with Tonio, and Rocco still had scars from the beating. Things between son and father went downhill from there.

That was not the worst, however, of the disasters that came from the Fantini's Russian adventure. Tonio's activities might have been off the government's radar, but it was not off the radar of the mafia families who divided the city. They tolerated Tonio's activities as long as he was just small time. He was even useful as an outlet for excess merchandise they had acquired, but when he moved into prostitution, he was infringing on their monopoly and that was not to be tolerated.

The police found Tonio with a bullet hole in the back of his head and his manhood removed. The girls were gone. The only thing left of the house was its foundation and the smoldering embers of what had been Rocco's home. Rocco had graduated from high school the week before. Now he had no home, no father, no clothes, and only the fifteen hundred dollars that he had accumulated from his own deals and had hidden under the floor of the toolshed in the small backyard. The fire had scorched the shed. It was still standing, however, and his money was still there. There was nothing to stick around for and plenty of reasons to get the hell out of town. The name Fantini was no longer welcomed in Roseville or, for that matter, anywhere else in New Jersey. Rocco bought a bus ticket and headed for Manchester.

He lived with Rose and her husband until he could find his own place. They had given him a job in their Italian Pizza House, which had become an institution in the small southern town. Alberto's Italian immigrant mom and pop opened the pizza place in the 1950s. This was Coffee County, Tennessee, and ethnic restaurants of any kind—Italian, Mexican, even Chinese—just didn't exist in the early '50s. The Pizza House's only competition were the catfish place and the meat-and-threes on the square. Eventually, franchises arrived—a Krystal, Kentucky Fried Chicken, and a Dairy Queen. The town continued to prosper and eventually the pizza chains opened, but the Italian Pizza House survived, having secured its position as the hangout among the town's teen crowd.

Rocco decided quickly that a job wasn't really for him—especially in a pizza place. He was handsome like his father with an olive complexion and dark wavy hair. He worked out regularly and his body showed it—broad shoulders, muscular arms, tight chest, size thirty-four waist, flat stomach, and, according to the girls, a nice set of buns.

What he did like about the pizza place was the good-looking women he met. A lot of them were searching for jobs as servers. Manchester was still a small town in 1995. The country was recovering from a recession and these farm girls, many of them drop-dead beautiful, had few career opportunities. Nor did they have very good marriage prospects. Yes, there were available high school sweethearts, but many of the girls had bigger dreams.

Those dreams did not fit with the available pool of small-town men.

Rocco was exotic. He was from New York City. At least, that's what he told the girls. It wasn't long before he moved in with one of the waitresses. If she had expected monogamy from Rocco, she was badly mistaken. Like his father, he sampled every willing female he met. He talked his way into their bedrooms with his big-city stories. He had them dreaming about the excitement of New York City and Jersey Shore glitz in the summertime.

Drugs were just beginning to reach rural America. Coke was like champagne is to liquor. It was glamorous, and all the glamorous people did it. Rocco got one of his high school buddies to bring him the white stuff down from New York. While Rocco didn't touch it, he made it available to his women. It wasn't long before they had to have it. Coke was expensive, so he added methamphetamine to his menu of drugs. Addiction was a powerful recruiting tool. Rocco began to grow his stable of prostitutes—sexy country girls hooked on drugs with just one way to finance their habit. And Sammie appeared to be another perfect candidate for his family of whores.

The bordello's only competition was in Nashville. Rocco had better stuff. You didn't have to go to Nashville or risk Nashville cops to get his. Music City and surrounding areas were cracking down on prostitution, but Rocco had learned his way around politically—all it took was a little money in the right pockets to keep the authorities away from his business.

Chapter 12

Bryan's Report

Bryan spoke urgently over Black Beauty's intercom. "Chief, I'll give you what we have," he said. "But in all honesty, you didn't give us a lot of time."

"Go," I said quickly. "I have even less time left so stick to the important stuff."

"Roger. First, the sheriff, Liberty Bass, is a good guy. Your name should be enough to get you in the door without a problem. We've done him some favors in the past—tracked down some bad people for him. In addition, you donated to his reelection campaign, which wasn't chicken feed."

I remembered talking to him on the phone, but couldn't remember meeting him in person.

"I met him a few months ago," said Bryan. "You and Mrs. Rollins had a conflict, so Mariko and I stood in for you two at the Tennessee GOP Statesmen's Dinner. He's tall and lean with a big smile. Comes off as a little 'country.' After talking to him for a few minutes, though, I realized he's nobody's fool. He's smart. Ex-military. Army Intelligence, I think. He's quite the celebrity around Coffee County. Goes by his first name only. Everyone just calls him Liberty and now, after the election, it's Sheriff Liberty."

"Thanks," I said. "The description will help if I have to track him down in person."

Bryan continued, moving on to the subject of the girl and her boyfriend.

"I'm downloading pictures and what little bio I have on the juveniles," he said. "But for your purposes, I think their ages are what's important. Both are under eighteen. They appear to have been good kids, but their grades have plummeted in the last year."

"That's a marker, isn't it?" I asked.

"I'm afraid so," said Bryan. "It usually means drugs or alcohol. As for the mom, stage IV colon cancer may be an understatement. The cancer has spread to her liver. She's undergoing the standard 5-FU protocol. One of these days we'll look back on the treatment of cancer the way we look back on 'bleeding' in the primitive days of medicine."

"I've been in her shoes," I said. "I need to get her on the experimental treatment program I was on—one that adds Tarceva to the usual protocol of 5-FU, Leucovorin, oxaliplatin, and Avastin. But that's something I can deal with after we take the girl home to her mother."

"Chief, if you have enough time, I'd like to bring you up-to-date on what we found out about the girl's father."

"Keep it short for now," I said.

Bryan explained how the father's death looked suspicious to a few people in the Boston PD. Our brain trust's

Big John still has friends over at his former employer, Metro Nashville's CSI division. According to Bryan, those friends checked with their counterparts in Boston's crime lab. A lab team had been dispatched to the site, but they were pulled back when the ruling *death by natural causes* came down. Big John said that some of the team was not entirely comfortable with that decision. The doctor was wearing two 75 microgram fentanyl patches on the upper portion of his right arm. First, that was a double dose of an already strong prescription, yet there was no known history of opioid use.

"You would have to be an experienced opioid user to take that much fentanyl without it suppressing your breathing," said Bryan. "It was strong enough to kill someone who had never taken the drug. What troubled them more was the position of the patches."

"How's that?" I asked.

"The dead man was right-handed, boss. Wouldn't you have expected him to use his right hand to position the patches on his left arm? He would have had to use his left hand to put them where they were—that was strange."

"Interesting, but we'll have to pursue that later," I said. "What about the stepdad?"

"We're still working on him. I don't have anything yet."

"Okay. When you have something, let me know."

"Will do. Chief, there's something else you should know."

"You have to make it quick," I said. "We're almost to the jail."

"It's about the mother."

"What's that?"

"She's done a stretch in rehab—for drugs."

I felt shocked. So shocked, in fact, that I couldn't quite think of what to say next. Bryan picked up on my silence.

"Apparently after giving birth to her daughter," he continued, "she suffered what today they call 'baby blues.' Some women just get over it after a few weeks or a couple of months without the need for any treatment. She didn't—or at least that's my understanding based on my reading of the medical records we managed to retrieve electronically. Her condition developed into a full-blown case of postpartum depression."

"She told me none of that," I said. "In fact, she left it completely out of an almost day-by-day timeline of her life. Why would she do that? Leaving this out is as close to a lie as one can get!"

"Chief, I'm not a woman," said Bryan, "but even as a man I can think of at least two innocent reasons not to tell you."

"Enlighten me!"

"First, she probably felt ashamed or embarrassed about it. This is motherhood we're talking about," said Bryan. "You've just brought a beautiful living being into the world. You're supposed to be happy, supposed to love this new little baby unconditionally. And you don't. And you wish it never happened."

Bryan was right, of course. It's not the kind of feeling you want to share on social media or with the father of your old friend.

"Second," continued Bryan, "when you start talking about a clinical diagnosis of depression, you're touching on mental illness. People don't like to share that kind of information either."

"But that was seventeen years ago!" I said.

"Yes, a lot of time has passed, but frankly, Chief, your friend's problem may have been even more serious. They don't come right out and say it in black and white—not in the structured part of the file, but based on the margin notes, she may have experienced a postpartum psychosis emergency. With treatment, the doctors brought her condition under control, taking it down to the depression diagnosis. In layman terms, Chief, at least for a short of time, Mom was way off her rocker."

"What about the drugs?" I asked quickly, realizing the time.

"Once they got the emergency under control, the records indicate that her treatment, for the most part, was put in the hands of a psychiatrist who started medicating her. The doctor put her on the normal meds for depression and anxiety but didn't stop there."

Bryan had discovered that they prescribed OxyContin for Glenda, which led to addiction and doctor shopping when her regular doctors started backing off on the dosage and number of pills they were prescribing.

"Can it get any worse?" I asked.

"I'm afraid so, Chief," said Bryan. "Boston's finest picked her up for impaired driving. That's how she wound up in rehab. The judge put her there."

I was concerned. Really concerned. I knew that recovering addicts don't always stay sober, especially under stress. If Glenda Adams was anything right now, she was under stress. By leaving this out of her storyline, she was deliberately hiding it. Now I had to question the rest of her story. She had told it in such detail, though, that I had to believe she was either being truthful, or was one hell-of-a-good liar. Bryan interrupted my thoughts.

"It's not just about the question of her trustworthiness," he said. "You also have to consider her mental stability. There is a strong correlation between mental illness—including depression—drug abuse, and addiction. The statistics on comorbidity—depression and addiction—are shocking."

I knew the numbers. I had to think, to organize my thoughts and come up with a plan. Bryan wanted to know what I was going to do.

"Right now I'm going to keep my mouth shut and go with your initial theory of 'innocent reasons' until there is evidence to the contrary. At the same time, I agree that we can no longer accept everything Glenda tells us at face value. Who was it that said 'trust but verify'? Well, it applies here."

"Ronald Reagan," Bryan said quickly before the line went dead.

Chapter 13

Call to the Sheriff

As soon as I hung up on Bryan, I realized we were stopped on the interstate.

"What's going on with the traffic?" I asked Tony. "I haven't seen any construction signs, but this is a parking lot. We're bumper-to-bumper on our side of I-24."

"It's Bonnaroo, Mr. R—you know, Tennessee's annual version of Woodstock. It's become a big deal."

"I thought that wasn't until June 13," I said, feeling frustrated. "This is what, the eleventh?"

"Right you are, Mr. R, but these are the veterans of the event," said Tony. "You have to arrive early to get a good spot."

Tony loved these kinds of facts. He reminded me that during Bonnaroo's four days, Manchester becomes Tennessee's largest city. Normally, our trip would have been a short drive from Franklin. Not today. Bonnaroo traffic—especially the RVs—was going to cost us another thirty or forty-five minutes, if we were lucky.

"Maybe we should have considered a helicopter," said Tony. "I think they have a pad at the jail."

"Do the best you can," I said. "I tell you what—why don't you take exit 111. We're coming up on it."

I knew Woodbury Highway would get us to US 41. The jail's address was 300 Hillsboro, which is also Highway 41. It might not have saved us any time, but it beat bumper-to-bumper on the interstate.

"While you're doing the driving, I'll call ahead and talk to Liberty," I said.

Reaching the sheriff by phone was not as easy as I expected. There were a lot of staff between me and the busy sheriff. Bonnaroo was too big an event for the local authorities to handle without help. The sheriff brought in volunteers and first responders from all over the state. The Tennessee Highway Patrol played a leading role handling the traffic and problems with motorists. Even the Feds were there with the DEA. There were always music lovers who wanted to live the Woodstock drug experience. Drugs were everywhere back then, so the DEA put people on the ground at Bonnaroo to identify the professional pushers. If that wasn't enough cause for confusion, any time you had that many people in one place, there were concerns about terrorists. Especially given the nearby location of the Air Force's Arnold Engineering Development Complex. Homeland Security had a small army of undercover characters trying to blend in with the festival crowd, some of whom were half-naked and drugged out. The sheriff was a very busy man right now; but I persevered and, finally, Liberty answered.

"Hello, Mark, just to let you know, I took the call because it's you. Whatever it is, if it will keep, let's table it until after this damn Bonnaroo craziness."

"It will only take a second, Sheriff," I said. "You have a young girl there, Samantha Miller. I'll be at the jail in thirty or forty-five minutes, and I'm hoping to take her home to her mother."

"I know about her, believe it or not," said the sheriff. "We're not charging her, so she's free to go. She's in the waiting area. I would just as soon not get into any details right now—too busy. If you want to know the circumstances surrounding our picking her up, I'll be glad to go over the details in a couple of weeks. Okay?"

"Great news!" I said. "I won't keep you. Good luck with the crazies."

"Thanks," he said with a chuckle. "I need luck—lots of it. As Biden said, 'This is a big f_ _ _ing deal!'"

After my brief conversation with the sheriff, I called Glenda to let her know about the results of my call. All we had to do now was get to 300 Hillsboro Boulevard and pick up our package, Samantha Miller, aka Sammie, and deposit her home safe and sound.

Chapter 14

Sammie's Ride

The public visitors' waiting room at the Coffee County Jail was a large, open area separated by a low wall from the more "business" side of jail activity. The wooden chairs were arranged theater-style, facing the low wall. Just inside the entrance was an information kiosk staffed by a deputy perched on a stool. Opposite the front doors on the other side of the room were the restrooms.

Just like in church, most of the visitors had opted for the back pew, finding seats farthest away from the information desk. Sammie had been steered to a chair directly in front of the information desk staffed by Lewis's cousin. Tom Lewis sat down in the chair next to her. He moved his chair closer. Their backs were turned toward the rest of the visitors. Except for the information officer, there were no other officers in sight.

Tom Lewis put on his best smile—the one he used when trying to pick up underage girls in the beer joints he frequented—and leaned toward Sammie, talking in almost a whisper.

"I'm here to help you, young lady. You waiting on someone?"

"The officer said my boyfriend is going to have to stay here," said Sammie. "I was with him. They called my mother. I talked to her, but she's sick. So, I don't know. I don't know."

"Well, you don't want to stay here for the rest of your life."

"No, no—I want to go home."

"Are you sick? You're shaking—sweating too."

Sammie wiped the palms of her hands on her jeans.

"I need my medicine," she said.

"Look, I've been there myself, and I know how to fix things."

Tom Lewis held out his hand. His open palm contained two 5 milligram Percocet pills.

"When you say medicine, don't you mean like these little round blue pills?"

"Oh, God," she whispered excitedly. "Thank you." Sammie reached for the pills, but Tom closed his hand back into a fist and said, "Not so fast, little lady."

Sammie's eyes pleaded with him. "I really need those. I don't feel well."

Tom smiled and said, "I'm willing to share. You can have *one*. The other is for me."

This time he offered her a pill that she quickly grabbed, popped in her mouth, and swallowed without saying anything.

Tom looked over his shoulder at the few visitors in the back of the room. They were dealing with their own problems. He knew from experience that people tended to avoid an officer talking to someone who might be a suspect.

They're not looking at us, he thought. *Don't want to get involved.*

He turned back to Sammie and said, "I know where we can get more Percs. Do you have any money?"

"No, but my mother would give me some money if I could get home."

"Where is home?"

"Franklin," she said. "But I don't think I want to go there yet."

"How much money can you get?"

Sammie was trying to calculate. The Percocet wasn't working yet so she had difficulty thinking straight. "Maybe fifty dollars."

Tom laughed under his breath. "You kidding? That won't even buy the gas to get you home."

"She's going to be so mad at me," said Sammie. "I really don't know what to do."

Although she was still scared, Sammie was beginning to feel better and think straighter.

"I can get you home and get you some more Percocet, but not without some money or some*thing* in exchange."

"Wait—I've got a debit card. Do you know somewhere I can get money with my debit card?"

"That works in ATMs, right?" asked Tom.

"Yes!" said Sammie who, for this first time all day, was beginning to feel okay.

"I know where you can get as many of the Blues as you want for five dollars a pill," said Tom. "And a friend of mine can drive you home for that fifty dollars you talked about."

"I don't want to go home," said Sammie. "Not yet. I'm in too much trouble."

"Well, you can't stay here. Ever been to Bonnaroo? I can hook you up with some people going there."

"I didn't think it was time yet," she said.

"Two more days before the gate opens, but people get there early. They camp out until it opens—have fun, take a few happy pills, maybe eat a mushroom or two. Ever had a mushroom?"

"No. That's kind of scary," said Sammie.

"Not with what you get around here," assured Tom. "They're safe as can be."

"But what about the campers—strangers, I mean. How can I be sure they aren't dangerous people?"

"Look at me—my uniform," said Tom, puffing out his chest. "I'm on the sheriff's team. If you can't trust a deputy, who can you trust?"

He smiled as widely as his skin would allow.

"I guess you're right," said Sammie. "Okay, but I need some things first."

"No problem. There's a Walmart right down the road. Say, do you have a cell phone?"

Sammie fiddled the phone out of her pocket and held it up.

"Why don't you call your mother and tell her you're going to Bonnaroo so she doesn't get scared and call out the cavalry to find you."

"I can't talk to her right now."

"Text her then," said Tom.

Sammie said okay and keyed in the following: *Don't worry. With friends going to Bonnaroo.*

Tom smiled. "Good, that should keep your mother happy. Here, take the other Blue. I've got more."

Sammie grabbed the pill and again popped it in her mouth without a word.

"Let me borrow your phone," said Tom. "I need to look up something about Bonnaroo and call my friends. What's your Apple ID?"

"Why do you need that?" asked Sammie.

"To get you a ticket to the event."

"Oh, yeah. It's j4#1776D."

Sammie handed him the phone.

Tom said, "I'll be right back as soon as I make a call to get you a pass to the event."

He turned his back and began walking away while pretending to make a call. He saw that the text hadn't transmitted to the girl's mother yet—poor cell connection inside the jail. Even though he had suggested it, Tom decided the text wasn't a smart idea. He deleted it. Better to leave the mother in the dark—keep her guessing. Then he changed Sammie's password and deactivated the phone. It was now useless. He put the disabled phone in his desk drawer. Then he used the phone on his desk to call Rocco and confirm the pickup. Smiling about his luck, he returned to Sammie.

"Got it all set up," he said proudly. "Oh, your battery was almost dead. I'm charging it for you. Feeling any better?"

"Yes, I'm okay now," said Sammie. "Thanks for the Percs."

"What are friends for?" said Tom. "A guy I know, Rocco, is going to drive you to the campsite just outside the event grounds. He'll be here in about five minutes. Cool guy. You'll like him—drives a fancy convertible. He'll pick you up outside."

"You've been so nice," said Sammie. "I don't know your name?"

"It's Tom. Now you have a fun time. I'm sure we'll meet again."

"I hope not," said Sammie more quickly than she intended. "I mean, I don't want to ever be back here—at the jail."

"No, I wouldn't want that for you either. But you owe me for those Percs. One of these days maybe you can give me something *I* need really bad."

Sammie didn't like the way Tom was looking at her. For the first time, he made her uncomfortable.

"I think I'll go outside and look for my ride."

Sammie walked out the door of the jail and down the steps just as a bright red Cadillac convertible pulled up. A smiling Rocco asked, "You Sammie?"

"Yes," she said, now feeling the full effect of the Percs. "Cool car!"

"Hop in and enjoy the ride."

She got in. Rocco drove away. The Percs were working and Sammie felt good. If they hadn't been working, some alarm bells might have gone off, but she was too mellow. Nothing seemed strange to her. The town's traffic lights all seemed to flash green.

Chapter 15

Carlos's Loose Ends

Carlos paced rapidly around the De La Cruz mansion lobby, waiting for his sister to return from a shopping trip. As soon as she cracked open the door, he pounced. "Sis, we've got trouble."

"So what's new, Carlos?" Lena asked sarcastically. "I'm beginning to think you should change your name to Brother Trouble. What new mess have you gotten us into now?"

"It's Yusuf," Carlos said, "the pill-head doctor we brought down from New England. I called his wife to see if she knew where the jerk was holing up. She doesn't. She thinks he has run out on his family obligations. It also seems the bitch's daughter is in trouble—sounds like drugs."

"Damn it, Carlos, why couldn't you just listen to me? This New England thing has been nothing but trouble from the get-go. What if the wife calls the police to report her missing old man? And, this trouble with the kid—

we don't need the attention. That's why we moved these people."

"I'm going to take care of it," said Carlos.

"*How?* How in God's name are you going to take care of it without making it even worse?"

"I don't know—burn their damn house down with them in it."

"I don't want you to do anything until we've agreed on what and how," said Lena. "You understand?"

"Look, sis, I don't need you telling me what I can and can't do. Just because you breathed air a few minutes before me doesn't make you the boss. I said I would take care of it, and I will!"

"That just isn't going to cut it anymore, little brother. This is *your* mess. Until we have it cleaned up, you're not on your own anymore. We're going to be like Siamese twins—bound together at the hip. You understand me?"

"No, I don't understand. But for the sake of a little peace, I'll play it your way—for now."

"Okay, good," said Lena, exhaling. "Now what about this missing jerk?"

"I don't know where he is," said Carlos. "Looks like he's on the run."

"From who and for what?"

"Atlantic City—it seems he didn't settle his debts. He made some token bullshit payment on his IOUs, but that's all. Our friends want their damn money. All of it, and they play rough."

"So why doesn't he just cough up the dough?" asked Lena. "Doesn't he know you can't stiff those people? Is he that stupid?"

Carlos shrugged his shoulders and said, "The money is gone—his dough from the clinic deal and a chunk of his wife's money. The guy is a compulsive gambler. He found somewhere else to lose it before my friends could get theirs."

"So, maybe they find him and solve our problem," said Lena. "At least that part of the problem."

"I don't think it's that simple."

"What do you mean?"

"They're blaming us."

Lena looked as if Carlos had just kicked her in the shin.

"Why?" she practically screamed. "Bullshit. What did we do?"

"We didn't do anything, but that doesn't change things," said Carlos. "We did the deal as a favor to those guys. For some reason, they seem to think we should have made sure that the doctor paid off his debts. Like, they consider it our fault that we let him stiff them again."

"Why are you mixed up with these people?" asked Lena. "We have a good thing going, and we don't need any dealings with the mob—at least, not anymore. Not since we got out of the illegal business. So, who are you trying to be anyway? Scarface or something? Don't ever forget what happened to those badasses in the end. They got killed or died in jail. You need to listen to me."

"Okay, okay," said Carlos. "What the hell do you want me to do or not do? At this point, you want it fixed, but you don't want me to do this or that. How can I fix the shit if you keep telling me what *not* to do?"

"I want you to do what you said and take care of it," hissed Lena. "Either find the doctor and turn him over to these people or, hell, better yet, just pay them off. It can't be that much. Just pay them."

"Like I said, it just isn't that simple," said Carlos. "We can't pay the doc's bill. If we do, we look like we're afraid of them. If we act scared of these people or pay them off, they'll think they can own us. Push us around—muscle their way in on our business."

"Then find the asshole doctor and turn him over," said Lena. "Let them do whatever they want. I hope they kill him."

"You don't know these people; that won't resolve the issue. They'll still blame us."

"Okay, genius, how do *you* propose to resolve this?"

"We have to get their money for them," said Carlos. "But it can't look like it came from us. If we can't find the doctor, we'll strong-arm the wife. Even if that doesn't work, it will *look* like it did. Hell, as you said, we could supply the money. It's only about a million. We just have to look like we're making good on our part. You know, insisting that the doctor or his wife pay up."

Carlos looked satisfied with his plan. Lena seemed less than convinced.

"I don't like involving the wife," she said. "Find the damn doctor."

Lena figured a pill head and a compulsive gambler should be easy to find. It was a matter of locating where he got his stuff and where he played. She also figured they had better find him first—before the Atlantic City people got him and discovered he was a dry hole.

"Carlos, this is serious shit," said Lena. "You're a risk to everything we built and to me personally. You need to cut any ties with those people in Atlantic City and clean up this New England mess. If you screw up, I'm not going to save your ass. In fact, I'll do whatever is necessary to save me and our business. Do you understand?"

"I would never rat you out," said Carlos.

"I don't want you to misunderstand," said Lena in a quiet but serious voice. "I will protect myself from your stupidity."

"I think you're trying to tell me that you would kill your own little brother to save yourself."

"Damn right, if it comes to that," said Lena. "Don't ever forget it. I suspect you would do the same."

"You are one mean bitch," said Carlos with a laugh. "So how is this for a plan?"

Carlos went on to suggest that he would find the doctor, beat his brains out, show pictures of his bruised and busted body to the Atlantic City guys, and pay them off—maybe even put a little blood on some of the money just for fun. He would then take the doctor out where the sharks feed and toss him in with the little fishes.

"How does that sound?" asked Carlos. "Okay with you, big sister?"

"You're being cute, Carlos. But, yes, that is exactly what you are going to do. Make it happen, goddammit. Make it happen!"

"Then what?" he asked. "What do you want me to do with the wife and kid?"

"I liked your idea," said Lena. When the time is right, burn them down. Burn the house with them in it. I want it all gone. I want nothing left—not even a single piece of paper that might lead back to us. It needs to be big. I don't want any pissant arson job that the fire department can put out before everything is destroyed."

"I know a guy that can make that happen—a gas explosion. It'll be a pile of charcoal before the fire department can even get there."

"Then what, dear brother? We would just replace one loose end with another one—the guy who does the job for us."

"I know how it's done," said Carlos. "I'll do it myself."

"Okay, but remember what I said. Don't screw up, Carlos."

"I know," he said. "If I do, you'll get rid of the loose ends—namely me."

"Right, little brother—so don't screw up!"

As Carlos turned on his heels and marched out of the mansion, Lena knew she could never simply kill her brother. She needed him alive; her life depended on it. She would not hesitate to sacrifice his life for hers, but that needed to happen in an operating room, not on the streets. She needed to start thinking about a way to preserve him—keep him safe and keep him from doing something stupid enough to bring everything crashing down. Yes, *preserve*—that was the right word.

Chapter 16

Manchester Jail

Tony peeled Black Beauty into the parking lot of the Coffee County jail.

"We finally made it, Mr. R," he said. "Sorry it took so long."

"It's okay," I said. "I plan to be here only long enough to pick up our passenger, so just pull up to the front entrance and stay close."

"Roger—just as soon as that convertible is out of our way."

"My plan is to deliver the girl to her mother pronto," I said.

As soon as the car came to a stop, I bolted out and ran up the fifteen steps to the entrance. For some reason, I felt something in my gut that I didn't like. A sinking. A kind of knot.

Once inside the jail I saw what looked like a hospital waiting room. I was surprised by the lack of security. Then I realized that there was plenty of police presence on the far side of the room. A wall of personnel and airport-like scanning equipment separated the visitors from the business portion of the jail.

There were ten or twelve visitors in the area—people not in uniform. But no scared young woman sitting alone. There were grandmother- and grandfather-types along with middle-aged men in work clothes. I spotted an information desk manned by a uniformed guard who was trying to satisfy a very pregnant, teary-eyed young woman with his boilerplate answers. Like many information desks, the person behind this one provided little helpful information. The young woman gave up and headed back to her seat. I was next in line.

"Yes, sir," he said without looking up. "Can I help you?"

"I'm here to pick up a young lady," I said. "Samantha Miller. She goes by Sammie."

The guard flipped through several sheets of printed pages on a clipboard, shook his head, and said, "Let me check the computer."

I waited as he two-fingered his way across the keyboard. He looked up and said, "Sorry, I don't see anyone by that name in our custody."

"I called about forty-five minutes ago and talked to Sheriff Liberty," I said. "She was brought in earlier with a young man, Billy Underwood. You might have him as William or something."

The guard went back to working on his computer. "Yes, I see an Underwood. We do have him, but there is nothing about anyone else—no girl."

"The sheriff said that you were not charging Miss Miller so I could pick her up and take her home."

"I'm sorry, Mister—?"

"Rollins, Mark Rollins," I said. "That's my name. Now, if you don't mind, what's yours?"

"Jimmy Lee Wilson," he said without meeting my gaze. "I wish I could help you, Mr. Rollins, but there's nothing in my computer about the girl you're looking for."

"I would like to talk to the sheriff," I said.

"He's not here. Your best bet, Mr. Rollins, is to call his office and talk to his secretary or his chief deputy."

"Look, Mr. Wilson, Sheriff Liberty said Sammie would be in the visitors' waiting room. This is the waiting room, is it not?"

"Yes sir, it is."

"This is the *only* visitors' waiting room, right?"

"Yessir."

"Then where is she, Mr. Wilson?"

"I don't keep up with who comes and goes—maybe the restrooms..."

"Where are they?" I asked impatiently.

Wilson pointed. "Over there, if you want to check."

I did. After knocking and getting no answer, I went into the ladies room and checked all the stalls. There was no Sammie and, thankfully, no one else. That knotted feeling in my gut was getting tighter—a thousand times tighter. I had told Glenda I would be bringing her daughter home. I sure as hell wasn't looking forward to my next call to her.

The guard looked up from the papers he had been studying as I returned to his desk. "Any luck?"

My reply was short. "No."

"I'm sorry, mister," he said. "But if you're looking for answers, I don't have any for you. I can't tell you if she was or was not here. That just isn't my job. I don't keep up with the comings and goings."

Jimmy Lee Wilson was smiling at me, but it was a self-satisfied smile, and I didn't like it. While I was checking out the ladies restroom, he had been deciding what to say to make me give up and go away. It wasn't going to work. I wasn't going to give up—ever.

"Jimmy, my boy, you haven't even asked me what she looks like," I said. "So how do you know if she was or wasn't here?"

He swallowed, and I could tell the gears were turning in his head, but the best he could come up with was, "Okay, what does she look like?"

"She's an attractive seventeen-year-old girl that would have been hard for you to ignore."

"Sorry, sir, I don't recall seeing anyone like that," he said. "If she's that good looking, I'm sorry I missed her."

The guard was lying; I was sure of it. The more I questioned him, the more evasive his body language had become. Except for his one smiling attempt to dismiss me, he had not been able to look me in the eye. His gaze went elsewhere—the ceiling, the floor, the stack of papers littering his desk. He was either wishing he were somewhere else or that someone would intervene so he could hand me off. One way or the other, he wanted to get away from my questions. And me.

I decided to give him some time to think while I asked some of the people in the waiting room about Sammie. Most didn't speak English and my Spanish wasn't up to the job; however, the pregnant mother stopped crying long enough to ask, "Are you a lawyer?"

"No," I said. "I'm looking for someone—a young girl, seventeen years old and alone. Have you seen her?"

"I think so," said the woman. "If it was her, she was sitting over there."

She pointed to chairs that were directly in front of the information desk. If it were Sammie, she would have been clearly visible to Mr. Jimmy Lee Wilson. The only thing between her chair and the information desk would have been the open space that served as a wide aisle.

The mother continued. "She was talking to one of the guards when I last saw her. They were huddled together, talking real close so they couldn't be overheard. I wasn't sure if she was in trouble, or a witness to something, but whatever it was, it looked like police business. I don't know what happened to her. I went to the restroom and she wasn't here when I came back. She must have left."

"How long ago was that?" I asked.

"Well, when I came out of the restroom I went back to the information desk to find out if they could tell me anything new about my husband and that was when you came in."

"You're saying she left just minutes before I arrived?"

"Yes, she must have."

"Thank you," I said. "You've been very helpful to me. Why did you ask if I was a lawyer?"

"They arrested my husband," she said as something like a shadow returned to her face. "He didn't do anything wrong. He lost his job and some people were trying to take our car. He got in a fight and they arrested him."

"Sounds like they were repossessing the car," I said. "If that was the case, then they had the legal right to take it.

Unfortunately, that means that in the eyes of the law your husband did do something wrong. But I know someone who can help you. What's your name?"

"Kathie Hicks Fuston," she said.

I gave Kathie my card after writing down the phone number for my attorney.

"You call Curtis Howard as soon as your husband has been processed," I said. "Mr. Howard will be expecting your call. What kind of work does your husband do, Kathie?"

A hint of pride crept into her voice. "He was in the Marines and has only been home for a year."

"When all this is cleared up, have him call me," I said. "I know people in the security business that might be looking for someone with his experience."

"Thank you!" she cried. "You don't know what this means to me. There was no one to help us. I feel like things are going be okay now."

"We'll make them okay," I said. "Don't worry."

I went straight back to information desk and placed both fists in front of Jimmy Lee Wilson and leaned in.

"You're lying to me," I said. "I'm going to give you one chance to come clean and tell me what I need to know. If you don't, and if you don't do it now, you are going to lose your job—and if anything has happened to that young girl, you are going to lose a lot more than a job."

The guard flinched, but he was too dumb to make the right decision. He was sticking to his story.

"Mister, I'll say it again. It's not my job to keep up with people who are not in our custody. If she was here and left, that's no concern of mine. People out here come and go; I'm not responsible for keeping up with them."

I looked around the room and spotted what I was hoping for—cameras. It was obvious that the waiting room and the entry door were being monitored from several different angles. I hoped that all of it was being recorded. I went back to Mrs. Fuston.

"Kathie, you said that the girl I'm looking for was talking to a guard."

"Yes," she said.

"Do you know which one?"

"No."

"Was it the guard at the information desk?" I asked, hoping to catch Jimmy redhanded.

"No. But they knew each other."

"How do you know that?" I asked.

"Just the way they treated each other," she said. "You know, waving and high-five signs—things like that. I think she talked to him too."

"Have you seen him since? I mean the guard that was talking to Sammie?"

"That was her name?" she asked with genuine concern.

"Yes, that's what people call her," I said.

"No, I haven't seen him."

"Would you remember him if I showed you a picture of all the guards?"

"I would try, but I don't think so," she said. "I just saw the uniform. I didn't really study his face."

"Okay, thanks again," I said.

There was nothing else for me to do here. If I was going to find Sammie, and I sure as hell planned to, I needed

Bryan's help and I needed it fast. The monitors. Hard evidence.

On my way out, I stopped at the information desk one last time. I put my business card on the desk, looked Wilson in the eye, pointed to the card, and said, "I suggest you think carefully about your future, young man. If you decide you want one, call me."

I left the building. Tony was waiting for me in the car.

Chapter 17

Where Is She?

I anticipated Tony's question before I got in.

"Where's the girl?" he asked.

"I'll be damned if I know, Tony. She's missing. Somebody in there sure as hell knows what happened to her, and I'm going to find out who."

"What *do* we do now, Mr. R?" asked Tony. "You want to head back to the WHC?"

"No. For now, just drive around the city while I try to figure some things out."

"Will do."

Tony pulled away from the jail and I dialed Bryan. In less than a second, I heard his familiar, "What's up, Chief?"

"That's what I want to know, Bryan," I said. "I made it to the jail, but there was no Samantha Miller waiting for me."

I told him that she had been there and that one of the civilians in the visitors' area confirmed it. But, of course, the guard overseeing the visitors' area was uncooperative. Claimed he saw no one like Sammie.

"He's lying," I said. "I don't like this, Bryan. She's just a seventeen-year-old girl. If she has gotten herself messed up with drugs, she might be going through withdrawal. Sammie Miller is an unaccompanied teenage girl and, if she's not thinking straight, we have a very dangerous situation."

"Are you afraid someone may have abducted her?" asked Bryan.

"I doubt anyone dragged her out of the visitor's area against her will," I said. "That would have definitely been noticed. She didn't have any means of transportation on her own. So, what if someone offered her a ride—someone she considered a nice person doing a good deed?"

It was a new theory, but I had to consider the location and clientele. A jailhouse isn't typically full of Good Samaritans. If she got in a car with someone, she may have just gotten herself in even more trouble.

"Are you concerned about human trafficking?" asked Bryan, reading my mind.

"Damn right!" I said.

Both Bryan and I knew that hundreds of teenage girls disappear every day. Bad characters get them addicted and use drugs to turn them into prostitutes. It's not just human trafficking; it's sex trafficking. What really set off all my alarm bells in the jail was the way the guard avoided giving me straight answers.

"Something isn't right," I said. "I'm afraid that spells trouble for the girl. Bryan, there are cameras everywhere in the visitors' area of the jail. I need you to hack their system and find out what happened to Sammie."

"What about her cell phone, Chief?" asked Bryan.

"I've tried calling her. It goes straight to voice mail."

"Give me the number," said Bryan. "Let me see what I can do to locate the phone."

"It's a 617 area code. She's apparently still using her Quincy, Massachusetts, phone. I'm texting the number to you now."

"Got it, Chief. Anything else I can do for you?"

"Tell me something about the stepfather," I said, wishing for some kind of break. "Any luck finding him?"

"The best we've been able to do, so far, is collect breadcrumbs—things we can use to track him," said Bryan. "The man is either dead or he's trying to drop off the radar."

Bryan and the WHC brain trust knew that people have figured out that their cell phone is a big *here I am* sign. The people who don't want to be found ditch their phones. When they do, my crew starts looking for their breadcrumbs—their behavioral and digital signatures. Things like their ID numbers, passport numbers, car licenses, credit cards, club memberships, vendor loyalty programs with hotels, rental cars, airlines, etc.

For example, Bryan told me he hacked his way inside the missing doctor's Internet provider. From there, he identified his digital habits—Internet sites he visited regularly as well as merchandise and services he had the habit of buying. The guy had been buying St. Johns Bay Rum cologne for years—his favorite, I guess. According to Bryan, it's imported. He buys it from the St. Johns Company via the Internet, so Bryan said he put a watch on that vendor's e-commerce site. He's also doing this for sixteen other products from a variety of vendors—things like his gourmet coffee preference. Now, we'll monitor Internet activity looking for a pattern that includes sites he frequents, products he habitually purchases, and variations on user names and passwords he has previously used.

"We've collected a lot of breadcrumb identifiers that we're now following," said Bryan. "Unfortunately, they haven't led us to our guy yet. Which leads me back to the hypothesis that he is either dead or dropped off the radar on purpose and is damn good at it."

"Maybe they're together," I suggested. "Her stepfather may have gone to the jail and gotten her. We can't rule that out."

"Would that be good or bad?" asked Bryan.

"I honestly don't know," I said. "It's a possibility we need to consider, that's all. There's one thing that we know for certain: he was moved here by his employer to be the supervising physician for some pain clinics in the Middle Tennessee area."

I hoped Bryan had been able to identify the location of those clinics. Maybe I could make a surprise visit or two. Who knows? I might get lucky. Thankfully he was one step ahead.

"Got it for you, Chief," said Bryan. "Two of the clinics are near your present location. One of them is in Manchester on Hillsboro Boulevard. The other has a Tullahoma address, but its actual location is outside the city."

According to Bryan, both were part of GCPM, Inc.—Good Comfort Pain Management. He quickly sent the

GPS coordinates for both locations to my navigation system.

"Got 'em, Mr. R," said Tony from the driver's seat. "We're only about seven miles from the Manchester address. Shall I head that way?"

"Yes, Tony. But let's first drive by the facility slowly—make a couple of passes."

"I got you," said Tony. "You want to case the place."

"Exactly," I said. "And Bryan, remember your top job is to find out what the cameras in the jail's visitors' area recorded. Find out what happened to Sammie for me. Make that and tracing Sammie's cell phone your top priorities. Call me the minute you have answers. I'm not looking forward to calling the mother with more mysteries."

"Will do, Chief," he said. "But there's one more thing you might want to check out."

"What's that?" I asked.

"Bonnaroo!" said Bryan. "I mean, she *is* a teenager. The event is a big draw for the teen crowd. You're near the site. She might have hooked up with someone going to the event. It could just be an innocent but stupid decision on her part."

He was right, of course. It *would* be stupid. But because Tony reminded me that tailgater-types are already partying in advance of Bonnaroo, we couldn't ignore the possibility.

"I'll do what I can to check it out," I said. "You do the same. There must be cameras all around Bonnaroo, not to mention the TDOT cameras on the roads. I have some digital photos of the girl; I'm sending those to you right now. Use facial recognition software and start auto-scanning any camera feeds from the vicinity."

"Will do, Chief," said Bryan.

We have a lot of friends at the Tennessee Department of Transportation. When they needed it, we've used our systems to monitor their statewide camera network in real time, and at the same time looked back twenty-four hours. We can identify license numbers, auto or truck descriptions, and facial patterns. They don't have our kind of capability in-house. We work together, which meant we shouldn't have a problem looking for Sammie on TDOT cameras."

"Good hunting," I said. "I hope you come up with something before I have to talk to her mother."

Chapter 18

Call from the Hospital

I had been off the phone with Bryan for less than three minutes when an incoming call from Centennial Hospital appeared on the car's communication display. *Why would I get a call from a hospital?* I wondered. Then it struck me—Sammie. She could be hurt. I took the call immediately.

"Hello, this is Mark Rollins."

"Mark, it's Glenda. I hadn't heard from you. Do you have Samantha?"

"In a minute," I said. "First, why are you calling from Centennial?"

In a frenzied monologue Glenda said she had woken up in the hospital, apparently having blacked out. She wears one of those medical tracking devices. The doctor said she had a reaction to her chemo. That's another thing she wears—a device that pumps chemicals into her body continuously.

"They want to keep me in the hospital for a couple of days until they've adjusted my medications," she said. "What about Sammie? I've been trying to call her but her cell phone isn't working."

"I know," I said. "I've called her, too, with the same result."

"But, you got her, right?"

"I'm sorry, Glenda, but she wasn't at the jail when I got there," I said. "No one seems to know where she went."

For a second I heard nothing on the other line.

Suddenly, Glenda cried out, "Mark, you have to find her!"

"I'm trying," I said. "Is there a chance she might have met up with her stepfather?"

"No!" she screamed. "That's *impossible*. There's not a chance of that."

"Why impossible?" I asked, feeling a little rattled by her response. "What makes you say that?"

"Well, at least I don't think so," she said, quickly calming down. "I mean, how would he know where to find her?"

"Could she have called him?" I asked.

"I can't imagine her doing that. She and Yusuf weren't close."

"You mean they were estranged?"

"It's not like that," Glenda said. "But they weren't pals either. I have no idea where he is and I certainly don't think Sammie does."

"What about the people your husband works for?" I asked. "I mean, the guy's a doctor. I know you think he's run out on you, but I assume he's still working in his profession. Couldn't she have gotten in touch with him through the clinics?"

Again, Glenda practically yelled into the phone, "He didn't just run out on us, Mark!"

She said a man named Carlos had called her yesterday insisting he was the investor that both Yusuf and her first husband dealt with. It was his group that purchased the clinic. He was pumping her for information. *When did she talk to Yusuf last? Where was he when she talked to him? Did he usually call her every day?*

"They don't know where he is either," she said.

"Glenda, do you think Yusuf could be hiding from those people?"

"I don't know," she said. "All I know is that my husband has disappeared. And frankly, I don't give a shit!"

"This Carlos, have you ever met him?" I asked.

"I remember meeting a man that might have been him back in Quincy, but I only knew him by his last name, De La Cruz. I can't be sure he's the same man."

I asked Glenda if she could produce the names and phone numbers of all the investors. I needed everything she knew about the group, including the phone number for this man named Carlos.

"As soon as they let me go home, I can give you everything I have for what it's worth," she said. "I don't have much that will help you. That's where the records are—my home."

"Would it be okay if I sent someone to your house to retrieve those records?" I asked.

"No!" she said quickly. Perhaps too quickly. "Don't do that. You wouldn't know where to look. And I'm not even sure I have anything that would be useful to you anyway."

I tried to reassure her.

"Our people are pretty good at finding things," I said. "It might be important. I don't like the idea of waiting until you are released from the hospital."

She remained resistant, saying she didn't want strangers going through her things.

"I'm having trouble thinking right now," she admitted. "I just don't feel right. But I know there is nothing there that will help you find Sammie and that's the only thing I can think about right now."

"We will find her," I said, making another promise I hoped I could keep.

She didn't answer. I heard the phone receiver fall and hit the floor.

I quickly punched Centennial into the communication system, which dialed the main number for the hospital. I noted that the Centennial call from Glenda had come from room 423, according to the info on the communication system display. The operator answered, "Centennial Hospital. How may I direct your call?"

"This is an emergency," I said. "I was talking to the patient in room 423 and—" In the middle of my explanation, the original call that I had kept open on my end came alive. "Hello, hello?" But it wasn't Glenda's voice.

I disconnected my call with the hospital operator and answered. "Yes? This is Mark Rollins. Is everything okay? I was talking to the patient, and she may have fainted."

The voice on the other end said, "I'm her nurse, and we are looking after her now. I think the morphine took effect and the poor thing just dozed off."

"Morphine?" I asked. "I take it she's in pain."

"Are you a member of the family?"

"No, I'm a friend," I said. "But I'm all she's got right now."

"You asked about pain," said the nurse. "The answer is yes, and it's only going to get worse for the time she has remaining. Her signs are okay now, but she's so opioid tolerant that we're having a difficult time getting her dosage right."

The nurse explained that increased tolerance is typical for people being treated for pain.

"She's resting and I have to go now," said the nurse. "You can see her during visiting hours."

The phone went dead.

I stared at the car's console. I didn't understand Glenda's position at all. Why was she so adamant about our not going to her house? That didn't make sense to me. And, I was pretty sure the problem with her tolerance to opioids wasn't just due to pain treatments. Tony interrupted my thoughts, „We're coming up on the clinic now, Mr. R."

I looked out the window. What I saw didn't look like any medical clinic I had seen. It looked like a double-wide—two trailer facilities hooked together to form a single building. There was a ramp running up one side to the front door and a line of people snaking from the door to the parking lot. The parking lot area was much bigger than you would have expected for such a small facility, and it was overflowing with cars, RVs, pickup trucks, and SUVs. I scanned the license plates: Tennessee, Kentucky, Indiana, plus a smattering of other states. People were smoking, and I suspected it was not all tobacco. There were small groups of people loitering in what little shade was available. Some were drinking from ambiguous bottles hidden in brown paper bags.

"What the hell is this?" I asked Tony.

"Got me, Mr. R. You want me to park and ask around?"

"Look over there," I said, pointing to one of the sheriff's cars under a tree.

"He's probably off duty, moonlighting as private security," said Tony of the skinny officer leaning against the hood. "That's how a lot of those guys supplement their income."

"There aren't many cars like Black Beauty in that parking lot," I said. "Drive around the block. I'll take the driver's seat and then let you out here. See what you can find out. I'll pick you up in about twenty minutes."

"I'll do my best, Mr. R."

Around the block, Tony opened the door and hopped out into the baking sun.

Chapter 19

Casing the Clinic

Tony was waiting near the street as I pulled up. I had kept Black Beauty out of sight, concerned that it might attract too much attention given the dilapidated condition of most vehicles in the clinic parking lot. As I came to a stop, Tony wasted no time getting into the front passenger seat. I moved just as quickly to get us away from curious eyes. I didn't want to gain the attention of the security guard who so far had ignored us in favor of the *Sports Illustrated* magazine he was reading as he leaned against his car. I wanted to keep it that way.

"What did you find out?" I asked.

"From what I've read, that place is your standard-issue pill mill," said Tony. "You walk in, see a doctor, pay $250 or so for a perfunctory exam, and walk out with a prescription. At least that's what my fellow druggies told me." Tony smiled.

"'They thought you were one of them?" I asked.

Tony said he fit right in, and perhaps he was right. He had messed up his hair, ditched the black tie, untucked his shirt, and rubbed a little dirt on his pants.

"That seemed to be enough to make me one of them," he said. "Although I might have still looked a little too clean."

"That was good thinking," I said. "Did you find out what drugs they wanted prescriptions for?"

"Well, to be honest, Mr. R, most of the time I just had to smile and wave. I acted as if I knew what they were talking about, but most of it was over my head. They weren't exactly using medical terms."

I went down the list of my own drug knowledge, rattling through names like 80s, O-Bombs, Bennies, Roxi, 40-Bar, Goofballs, Blues, Cotton, Percs, Stop Signs, 512s, etc. Tony nodded at most.

"Some of the guys were laughing and talking about their Holy Trinity," said Tony.

The slang, of course, was just the street names for drugs like Xanax, OxyContin, Percocet, and Roxicodone. Stop Signs and O-Bombs were the same things, Opana, which is an OxyContin-like med kicked up a notch.

I say notch, but it's more than that. When OxyContin isn't doing the job any more, Opana is their next step. It's a new form of opiate with twice the strength of OxyContin and, unfortunately, it can be crushed and chewed or even injected."

"What about that Holy Trinity, Mr. R? I don't think it has anything to do with church."

"The Holy Trinity is a cocktail," I explained. "Three pills taken together—OxyContin, Xanax, and Soma or carisoprodol."

Take away the Holy part and you have The Trinity—hydrocodone replaces OxyContin but you still have the Xanax and Soma. Hydrocodone is also called Vicodin and Lortab. On the street, I told Tony, it is usually referred to as hydros or vics."

"How come you know so much about this stuff, Mr. R?"

I told Tony that I was once a user thanks to those gifts that keep on giving—chemo and radiation. I had damaged nerves that sent out errant pain signals so I wore a fentanyl patch and took Oxycodone for breakthrough pain. Second, I was on the board of the Tennessee Drug Coalition for three years trying to deal with the opioid addiction epidemic in Tennessee. We had the second highest rate of prescriptions per person in the country. That's not a record to be proud of. At the same time, these were drugs needed for pain management. It's their *misuse* that was the problem—the diversion of pain medications to illegal recreational use.

"A lot of those people are there to get high," said Tony. "Not all, but a lot. What I don't understand, Mr. R, is why they go to a clinic. Why not just buy methamphetamines or some of the other stuff being cooked up in illegal labs? Wouldn't that be a cheaper way to get high?"

I reminded Tony that the street is a very dangerous place—you can be shot, knifed, raped, robbed, or arrested. And if that's not scary enough, the stuff coming out of meth houses and other makeshift labs can kill you.

"You have no idea what the stuff they are selling you really is," I said. "At least with the clinic, you know what you're getting. And all with an off-duty cop within arm's reach."

Tony went on to explain that many of the people in line looked like young college or college-dropout types. He wondered if they were getting the drugs for their own use or to share with friends. He said they didn't appear to be pushers out to make a billion dollars selling drugs on the street, although he did see a few older people there.

"When I asked them why they were at the clinic, they said their own doctors had cut them off from the pain medications they needed," he said. "They were there to get prescriptions for things like tramadol, hydrocodone, Oxycodone, and fentanyl."

The truth is, the medical profession hasn't come to grips with genuine pain management. Cancer patients have nerves firing off misdirected pain signals after surgery, chemo, and radiation. Honest doctors are so afraid of overprescribing these drugs that they go too far the other way. They leave people in chronic pain with no place to turn other than pill mills or the streets to get the medication they really need. I told Tony that was the exact drama he had just walked through.

Tony, in turn, tried his hand at sociology, trying to describe the different demographics he saw in the snaking line.

"It was easy to spot the people who were there to make money with drugs," he said. "Unlike the college-types out for fun and the old people who want their pain medicines, there were these gold-chain guys in designer jeans.

I figured the few fancy cars in the parking lot belonged to them."

I asked if he'd gotten any names. He said he had, like this guy Edwin Myers who was waiting to see the doctor. Tony said he picked out five or six more just like him.

"Here's the surprising part," said Tony. "This Myers guy said he's just paid help. He works for wholesalers."

"Tony, I guess you would call them the US version of mules," I said.

"Right, Mr. R. Although several of them didn't look like English was their first language."

"You mean they were Mexican or Latinos?"

"Well, a few were, but some looked Middle Eastern," Tony said. "But the Myers guy, the one I talked to, was every bit American."

It turned out that Myers was a bragger and wanted to regale Tony with as many details as he could. He said he made over half a million a year. That every three months he ran the circuit through Tennessee and Florida collecting scripts and getting them filled at cooperative pharmacies where he was a regular. With a kind of pride on his face, he told Tony that he used a different name and birthday at each clinic. Then he would take the drugs to his employer up north."

As Tony was relating the intel, I remembered a report on prescription drug trafficking abuse trends that came out of a conference in Brussels, Belgium. According to the report, buyers take their stuff to wholesalers in places like New England. The wholesaler supplies a constantly changing stable of retailers. A pill that costs less than a dollar can go for thirty or even fifty dollars on the street.

A ninety-day supply of hydro, about 540 pills, can yield around sixteen thousand dollars. Everyone along the way is making big money—the doctor, the doctor's investors, the mule, the wholesaler, and the retailer on the street. It all starts with a doctor willing to write the prescription.

"You wouldn't think they could get away with this stuff," I said. "The doctor must have a valid diagnosis. Get caught writing prescriptions for no legitimate purpose and you can lose your license."

Tony suggested that it starts before the doctor. That there must be patients willing to lie.

"The people I talked to coached me," he said. "Most of them go in complaining about back pain, but they said migraines work as well when you have a doctor looking for anything to hang his hat on."

The chicken or the egg thing. Which comes first, supply or demand?

"All this speculation is interesting," I said, "but it doesn't do anything to help us find Sammie. What about the doctor? Does he or she have a name?"

"They call him Dr. Mick," Tony said. "Nice looking young guy and he, too, is Middle Eastern according to one of the few women I talked to."

Tony, in fact, got more information in his brief time at the clinic than I could have imagined. The woman he referred to had approached him with a big smile on her face and reminded him a little of Mariko, he said—lots of tattoos and visible skin. Apparently, she got on a Harley bigger than she was and told Tony to look her up if he wanted some fun. Then gave him her business card."

Tony handed me the card. It listed her name, Sue Hadfield, address, phone number, and profession—*Dominatrix*.

"We need to get inside that clinic and have a talk with Dr. Mick," I said. "But, not today."

"Sure thing," said Tony. "Here's a good spot to pull over so I can take the driver's seat."

I hopped into the back seat with more than a few things to take care of. But first, I had to figure out everything I could on one "Dr. Mick."

Chapter 20

Crash, Explosion, Fire!

Tony and I were speeding down I-24 when I decided to head back to the WHC.

"There's nothing else for us around here," I said. "At least not for now. I have some thinking to do."

"Sure thing," said Tony, whose face I could see in the rearview mirror, deep in thought. "What do you think happened to the girl?"

"I don't know," I said. "Hopefully, Bryan can turn up something. If she's smart, she's left us some of those breadcrumbs Bryan is always talking about. Maybe the girl or the missing husband will call home. But, until we get something to go on, we're simply dead in the water."

Just then the car's communication console indicated an incoming call. I answered immediately.

"Mark, it's Sam Littleton."

"What's up, Sam?"

"Usually when we talk," he said, "you're calling me to ask for help. Well, this time I need to turn the tables—I need you."

"Sure, Sam. What can I do for the FBI today?"

"This is more in my Homeland Security capacity," he said. "We've caught wind of something big going down in the area, intel that seems to be pointing to an imminent attack..."

Before Sam could finish, Tony slammed on the brakes and I looked up just in time to see the flash and feel the explosion's impact. My entire field of view was a fireball and the fireball was expanding toward us. Tony threw the car in reverse and tried a three-sixty, but the shockwave hit us broadside, and the car started to roll parallel to oncoming traffic. A huge Mack truck skidded with locked brakes straight at us. Life shifted into slow motion just as the truck slammed its nose into my side of the car. Either the explosion had deafened me, or my mind had simply turned off the sound. Everything was silent as glass slow-motion exploded into millions of pieces, all flying straight at me. I could feel the heat of the truck's engine. I had the sense of the car being pushed sideways while at the same time I was moving toward the front of the truck. I fell hard—or was slammed—against the side of the car, which seemed to have merged with the front of the truck. Black Beauty was being crushed.

Finally, everything came to a stop. We were wedged between the truck and other cars. Those cars, in turn, had been pushed into the vehicles in front of them. I was sandwiched inside the car. My mind had turned the sound back on. I heard Tony groaning in pain and he said that he couldn't get out. He whispered that he could feel the heat of the fire somewhere in front of the car. We both saw that it was getting closer, leaping from one exploding car to the next. Tony was pressed against the console and the passenger seat. He was looking out the passenger-side window—or where the glass used to be. His seat had been turned by the impact of the Mack truck as it smashed into the side of the car. He said he couldn't move his right hand. There was no space for movement—his arms and legs were pinned. Someone outside the wreckage was screaming.

Then we heard sirens. Help was coming. If they could get to us in time.

"Tony, talk to me—where are you?" It was Bryan's voice. The communication system was still working. My brain began working, too, just barely, but not my voice—*yes, the air bags were deployed. Bryan would know that—Black Beauty would have automatically called for help.* Tony tried to talk and managed to utter, "Crash. I-24. Trapped. Fire coming toward us . . ."

"Help is on the way," shouted Bryan. "Hold on! And what about the Chief?"

I heard Tony say, "Don't know. Can't see him. No sound. Need out fast!"

"Fire, police, and ambulance are on their way," said Bryan. "You still there? Tony, talk to me! Talk to me!"

There was no answer. Tony had gone silent and, for perhaps the first time in my life, my words failed me too. Then everything went black.

Chapter 21

Sammie Wakes Up

Waking up came slow, encouraged by the sunlight coming through the thin curtain over the window. As Sammie opened her eyes and looked around, she tried to remember where she was. The words that formed in her head were, strangely, *Sammie, you aren't in Kansas anymore!* She remembered leaving the jail, but the space she was in, while larger, still felt like a jail cell. Across the room was a sink, toilet, and shower. There was no wall separating the toilet and shower from the rest of the room. A nightstand was next to the bed. A heavy-looking wooden chair was next to the only window. Also across the room, she could make out what looked like a closet, but it had no door. There was a door on the wall opposite the window, and it slowly opened. The man who emerged looked familiar, and then she remembered: He had given her a ride at the jail, but how did she get here? And where exactly was *here* anyway?

"Good, you're awake," the man said. "How are you feeling?"

"Where am I?"

"You're at my place. You passed out in the car."

"I don't remember," said Sammie, trying to shake the cobwebs from her mind.

"I was going to give you a ride to Nashville," the man said. "But you wanted to go to Bonnaroo. Don't you remember?"

"Who are you?" she asked.

"Rocco."

"You gave me something. You drugged me."

"No!" he said emphatically. "I gave you a Percocet, that's all."

Sammie looked under the covers and realized that she was undressed.

"Where are my clothes and my things? What did you do to me?"

"There are some other girls who live here," Rocco said. "They got you in bed and washed your clothes. Your things are in the closet when you're ready to get dressed."

"What about my phone?"

"I don't remember a phone."

"I had it at the jail," she pleaded.

"Maybe it's still there," said Rocco reassuringly. "I don't think you had a phone when I picked you up."

"Will you still take me to Nashville?"

"Yes, when you're ready, but some of the girls and I are going to drive to Bonnaroo. Why don't you go with us first? You know, have some fun."

Sammie was beginning to realize that she was very hungry, but maybe not for food. Her hands were shaking and she felt clammy.

It was as if Rocco read her mind. "Look, Sammie, I knew you were going to need something so I have a couple of Blues for you. He walked over and put two blue tablets on the nightstand. There's a glass by the sink. When you're dressed, come downstairs and have some breakfast. You can meet a few of the girls who live here. This week Nancy has kitchen duties. She'll fix some eggs and toast for you."

Rocco started for the door.

"Wait, what time is it?" asked Sammie.

"It's a little before nine," said Rocco. "We're going to leave for Bonnaroo about ten thirty, so you need to get a move on." He closed the door behind him as he left.

Sammie was starting to sweat. She rolled on her side facing the nightstand and stared at the two blue pills. Her hands were shaking so badly she had difficulty picking up the pills. She didn't wait for water. She put both in her mouth and tried to swallow. Her mouth was too dry. She threw her feet over the side of the bed and stood up on legs that weren't ready to support her. She fell back in a seated position on the bed. The pills would not go down. They were stuck in her dry throat. She was starting to panic—afraid of coughing them up and losing them. She managed to stand and get to the sink, but it was more like a controlled fall than walking or running. She got there and gripped the porcelain. The pills were melting in her mouth. Funny, she never thought about their taste before. It wasn't a good taste. She didn't wait for the glass to fill. It was enough. She brought the glass to her lips and drank.

The pills and their taste went down at last. She knew how long it would take before they did their work—before she would feel good again. It always took twenty minutes. She had timed it before. She was still holding onto the sink and realized she was naked. She was dazed, slightly delirious—*the shower—I'll take a shower and give the pills time.*

She stayed in the shower until the hot water started to give out then found a towel. She remembered the door. There was probably no lock. Someone could come in any minute. She needed to get some clothes on. She found her underthings, jeans, and blouse just as Rocco said she would and frantically put everything on. The pills were working. Things didn't seem so bad—maybe Bonnaroo would be fun. Nothing she did now could make things any worse. She thought about calling her mother, but she remembered she didn't have her phone. *That son of a bitch,* she thought. *The guard, he never gave it back to me!*

CHAPTER 22

Threat Level Bravo

Bryan was at his WHC desk, on hold, while Sam Littleton's secretary got him on the phone. With Mark in the hospital and Tony recovering, the crisis seemed over—no . . . not over, more like resting in the eye of a hurricane—the brief calm in the middle. Bryan knew he had to figure it out. Until the pieces were put together, the team, his WHC brain trust, had to remain on a crisis footing, ready for anything.

"Okay, Bryan. I'm here now," said Sam. "Sorry to keep you waiting."

"What the hell happened on that highway?" asked Bryan. "Was that a terrorist attack?"

"No, it doesn't look that way," said Sam. "We have some terrorist-related activity going on in the area, but this event just turned out to be a terrible accident. A propane truck and an empty Greyhound bus."

Sam explained that twelve people had been killed, but how it also could have been a lot worse. Mark could have easily been number thirteen, he said. The fireball was leapfrogging down the row of cars, and Mark's car was next in line when Sam's people got to him, just in time.

"Chalk that up as a victory," said Sam. "But we still don't know what the terrorists have in mind."

"So, you're convinced something is in the works?" asked Bryan.

"We are!" said Sam. "We had picked up chatter that at first was just making us nervous. That's why I was on the phone with Mark when it happened. We wanted his help to head off whatever the terrorists were planning. All we know is that something big appears to be in the works. We have some new intel that has moved us from nervous to afraid. We're already at threat level Bravo, and that means we have response teams deployed 24/7. That's also why we had the resources in the air that we were able to redirect to Mark."

"You have any idea of the target?" asked Bryan.

"Not really, but we're working on it, and we have made some progress," said Sam. From what we've picked up, the target is outside of Nashville—somewhere around the Manchester area. Two obvious bulls-eyes are Bonnaroo and Arnold Air Force Base."

"I can understand Bonnaroo," said Bryan. "It's a soft target and represents everything Jihadis hate about us—the Great Satan, you know. But why Arnold? Wouldn't that be a suicide mission? I mean, you can't storm the gates of a military base and not expect to be blown away."

"Right," said Sam. "But the terrorists inflict a lot of damage first. And that's what they want anyway—to die a martyr, take a shortcut to glory and the seventy-two virgins waiting for them to arrive."

"What are we talking about size-wise?" asked Bryan. "Is this a single madman, two or three guys, or an army?"

Sam said he was sure this wasn't just a lone wolf thing. Based on the chatter it had all the characteristics of a typical military-style raid.

"If they adhere to the pattern," said Sam, "it would involve a car bomb to create chaos or confusion, then a squad of three to five men with assault weapons who will kill as many people as they can before they go to meet their god."

"What makes you so sure of the count, Sam? Why three to five men?"

"More than five men would attract too much attention," said Sam. "Manchester is not a particularly hospitable place for Muslims. If people saw too many Middle Eastern men traveling or living together, we would hear about it."

Sam felt like the *"If you see something, say something"* campaign really was working. His gut was also telling him that he was looking for a bomber and three to four AK47 soldiers of Allah, and that the target was the Arnold base.

"That's why we still need you guys," he told Bryan. "We must find them before they attack or there's going to be hell to pay."

"What makes you think it's Arnold Air Force Base rather than Bonnaroo?"

"That's easy," said Sam. "Tell me—what weapon system has killed more of the terrorist leaders than any other?"

"UAVs of course," Bryan replied without hesitation.

"Right," said Sam. "Our Unmanned Aerial Vehicles like the Predator."

Sam explained how Arnold might be the Achilles heel of the country's manned and unmanned fighter fleet. The fact is, he said, nothing flies except through Arnold. It's the country's test laboratory for aircraft, spacecraft, and missiles. Arnold's motto is *test before flight*. Shut down the testing facilities, and you shut down the pipeline for new and modified aerial weapons. The deployment of fifth generation fighters would be put on hold—planes like the F35 Lightning II as well as further development of surveillance UAVs like the Global Hawk and the top secret RQ-180 would be delayed or even scrapped.

"We depend on those last two birds for long duration, high altitude eyes in the sky that can be stationed over a target area for around-the-clock monitoring," said Sam with a hint of pride in his voice. "They provide us with visual command of the battlefield, including those most at risk for terrorist activity."

Bryan shifted in his seat, checked the screens around his desk, and turned up the monitor's volume to better hear Sam's theory.

"When you stop and think about it," continued Sam, "Arnold is a logical target for radical terrorists. It's a way to deliver a blow to the very weapons that have decimated their leadership without going up against hardened targets. Rather than a head-on attack, they can accomplish their goal by striking our weaker flank. Arnold is a perfect target because no one has previously considered it at risk. It's not a hardened target—easy to hit with a big payoff."

Sam's point was clear. If the United States can't test, the terrorists will shut the door on new systems or modifications to the country's UAV fleet.

"But what if you're wrong?" asked Bryan. "What if it *is* Bonnaroo?"

"We have eyes on the roads, in the air, and on the ground," said Sam. "We'll do our best to keep anyone fitting the profile from even getting close to that big party. But face it, Bryan, if they hit Bonnaroo, it wouldn't have any military consequences. We have to focus our main effort on protecting the air base."

"I hope you're right," said Bryan. "It may be easier to protect the military base than a bunch of peaceniks reliving Woodstock. But if it turns out to be Bonnaroo, there's going to be a lot of dead people."

"I know, Bryan. But we're not going to let that happen."

Bryan had one last-minute thought. "You're basing your ideas on what the terrorists have been doing," he said. "But remember the lesson of 9/11—that *failure of imagination*. Maybe you need to think of how they might get to Arnold without their usual pattern of action."

"Thanks," said Sam. "We're not excluding anything—we are trying to be ready for all things, any time, in any form."

Chapter 23

Bryan Takes Command

The mood at the WHC was glum. The crash on I-24 had everyone shook up. The fatality count hit sixteen with more wounded. Mark and Tony were two of the first victims reached by first responders. In fact, their rescuers, a helicopter-based military medical team from Fort Campbell, had been in the air at the time of the disaster. Sam, on the phone with Mark when it happened, had immediately directed the medical team's helicopter to recover Rollins and his driver, Tony Caruso. Extraction had not been easy, but they got the job done. Tony's injuries were not life-threatening but required treatment and an overnight stay at Vanderbilt Hospital. Mark's condition was far more serious.

The three WHC principals, Bryan Gray, Mariko Lee, and an injured Tony Caruso, met in the second-floor repurposed conference room of the Women's Health Club—the control center, what Rollins called the "case room." Monitors dominated one wall, one of which displayed Sam Littleton's face. Sam was attending the meeting by video. Bryan was in charge as the case controller. Tony's arm was in a cast and he was nursing broken ribs.

With everyone present, Bryan opened the meeting.

"With the Chief in the hospital, it's up to us to pick up the pieces of this Sammie Miller situation," he said. "And at the same time, Sam Littleton has asked for our help regarding a possible terrorist plot."

Sam spoke up. "Bryan, you and I talked earlier about our terrorist concerns, but when it comes to this Sammie Miller issue, I'm in the dark. You have to bring me up-to-date."

Mariko nodded and said, "That goes for me too. I haven't been involved in either of these situations."

"Okay," said Bryan. "Let's deal with the Miller case first since that's what Mark was working on."

Bryan explained how an old friend of the Rollins family contacted Mark for help concerning her daughter, Sammie Miller. How the friend, Glenda Adams, had recently returned to Nashville with her second husband, Yusuf Arian, who would manage pain clinics around the state. He explained all the details—the missing husband, a missing Sammie, the threat of addiction—and made sure his colleagues understood how seriously Rollins had been pursuing the case.

Bryan paused. He was feeling a little drained. His throat was dry and he felt a little shaky. He reached for one of the water bottles in the center of the conference table, and as casually as he could, popped four of the pills he had stashed in his pants' pocket earlier in the morning.

Mariko noticed. "What's with the medicine?" she asked. "You coming down with something?"

"No," Bryan said quickly. "It's just something to help me stay awake. I didn't get much sleep last night."

"Bryan, be careful," said Mariko. "I don't know what you're taking, but some of those stay-awake things can really mess you up. We count on you for a lot. We need that big brain of yours working to keep us safe. We need you at the top of your game."

"Don't worry, Mariko," said Bryan. "These are just like a couple of extra cups of coffee—nothing more. Now, let's get on track. Has everyone followed me so far?"

Tony and Mariko had been listening intensely and taking notes—Mariko on an iPad with a keyboard and Tony, unable to easily use a keyboard with his broken arm, with pad and pencil. Tony already knew much of the story, but it was new territory for Mariko and Sam. Sam took no notes. He would have one of his rookie agents review the recording of the meeting and prepare a summary for his automated case book.

Sam spoke up, "I have two questions. Do you buy the no-affair thing? And, what brought them to Nashville?"

"Good questions," said Bryan. "I don't want to speculate about the affair yet. As for Nashville, that's where I was going next. For some reason, the Quincy clinic outside of Boston was sold again. The original purchaser was GCPM, Inc., or Good Comfort Pain Management. The corporation operates pain management clinics throughout Florida. They dumped the clinic, selling it to an individual doctor for practically no cash up front. Then GCPM moved the family, including Yusuf, Glenda, and the daughter, Samantha, to Nashville. According to the wife, Yusuf was to open and manage several pain centers in rural areas in Tennessee."

The crew took furious notes while Bryan paused, then continued describing the events at the Manchester jail and the girl's disappearance.

Tony interrupted, "I need to add that Mr. R had talked to the sheriff by phone prior to our arrival at the jail. The sheriff told him that the girl was not being charged with anything and Mark could collect her and take her home. So, we know for sure that she was there. Something happened to her between the time Mr. R talked to the sheriff and when we arrived about a half hour later."

Bryan took control again. "Thanks, Tony. That's the general background. The Chief's main objective was to recover the girl and get her to her mother. Frankly, though, based on the information we've assembled, the case isn't that simple. Let me lay out the task ahead."

Bryan explained his plan, starting with number 1: reopening the case of the dead partner, Raymond Miller, who he was convinced did not die of natural causes.

"There are likely to be nervous people willing to kill to protect their skin," he said. "If we turn to authorities in Massachusetts or elsewhere, given the current recorded cause of death, they are going think we are crying wolf over nothing."

Number 2: the missing second husband, who Bryan considered to be either dead or on the run.

"Which is it?" he asked. "That's a question we need to answer. If he's alive, we must find him and identify what he is running from. If he's dead, we need to determine the cause of death. If he has been murdered, we have a responsibility to bring the killer or killers to justice."

Number 3: because the Chief promised his family's friend that he would bring the girl home, Bryan said recovering Sammie was critical to everything.

Number 4: determine what happened to Sammie.

"We can't stop at just recovering the girl," said Bryan. "We need to know what happened to her and who was involved. If the people involved are up to no good, Mark would want us to shut them down."

Finally, number 5: the who/what/where/when and why of the pain clinics.

Bryan pounded the table. "Let's put them out of business!" he said. We know Florida has tried to shut down pain centers that prescribe legal drugs for recreational or illegal purposes. If Florida has run them out of their state, we don't want the bad guys relocating to ours."

Having finished his list, Bryan looked around the room, giving the rest of the team a chance to speak.

Mariko broke the short silence. "You sure about this?" she asked. "That's a lot to tackle. Why don't we just find the girl and let the authorities handle the rest?"

Sam interrupted, "When you get right down to it, Mariko, I *am* 'the authorities.' The FBI, the DEA, or the CIA probably have jurisdiction over various pieces, given our suspicions. We will do our part, I promise, but I could use your help. Bryan is right. This isn't a simple case of a missing girl. It's more like a mosaic—separate events that may form one picture. Somehow, they are all connected. Solve one and you solve the rest. You guys still have one big advantage over my people. You don't have to run to a judge to okay your every move. You can follow your gut. I have to follow the rules. Plus, Bryan's list doesn't touch on the terrorist aspects. That's where my team will direct most of its resources."

"Okay, I'm game," said Tony, still holding his broken arm. "Where do we start?"

"Before I lay out your assignments," said Bryan, "let me cover the terrorist business that Sam mentioned. That's Sam's priority one while ours is the Miller issue. In a nutshell, Sam is looking for a radical Islamic cell estimated to be five or fewer Middle Eastern men operating in the Manchester area. They suspect this group is planning an assault. The two most likely targets are Arnold Engineering on the air base or the Bonnaroo event. All Sam is asking us to do is to be on the lookout for these guys. If they congregate, they should be easy to spot. If you uncover anything that might lead Sam to these guys, get the info back to me and I'll be our liaison to the feds. Everyone got it?"

"We got it," said Mariko.

CHAPTER 24

Marching Orders

Bryan sat in Mark Rollins's usual place in the case room, ready to dole out the team's marching orders.

"With your wing clipped, Tony, it's best for you to stay close to home," he said. "I want you inside Glenda Adams's house today. Look for anything and everything that might give us a clue to the whereabouts of the missing husband."

"Is that okay with the woman?" asked Tony. "You have keys to the place?"

"No, I don't have keys, but I assume that won't be a problem for you. Ms. Adams is still in the hospital. I understand that she was reluctant to give Mark permission to enter the house without her being present. Frankly, that's precisely why I want you inside, and inside today."

"How careful do I need to be?" asked Tony.

"We don't actually have permission," said Bryan. "Even though she's been reluctant to give us access to the house, Mark told me he would try to work it out. As far as I'm concerned, I figure he got approval and that's what I'm telling you. But I'm not going to double check. We need in that house and I don't want to risk being told no-go. If you're discovered, play dumb—*you thought you had been cleared to enter the premises. You're on her team investigating the whereabouts of her missing husband. You don't have keys because Glenda Adams is hospitalized.*"

"Got it," said Tony. "But Bryan, I've been thinking about this terrorist business."

"What's on your mind?"

"One of the things that stood out when I was casing the pain clinic for Mark was the number of foreign looking men in the queue to get in to see the doctor," said Tony. "The more I've thought about it, some of them knew each other. They weren't together in line, but I remember eye contact and hand gestures. They were communicating. I mentioned to Mr. R that they could have been Middle Eastern. I thought it was unusual—the Middle Eastern part in the middle of rural Tennessee."

Sam had been mostly a silent observer until now. "That's useful info, Tony," he said. "If it's our group, they could be dealing drugs to finance their operation. I'll have a stakeout in place before the day ends. We will find out if they're our cell."

"Excellent job, Tony," said Bryan before turning his attention to Mariko.

"Okay, what's with the suit?" he asked with a chuckle.

Today Mariko was wearing a black vested, male skinny suit. The style was British avant-garde.

"I figured you might want me in Manchester to deal with the sheriff and his team," she said. "The sheriff is a politician and, as for his team, they all wear guns. Those kinds of people speak power to power. To get their attention you need gravitas. If I show up looking like a babe, they'll write me off. In this suit, I'm a high-priced attorney. I'll get their attention."

"Got it," said Bryan. "I'm guessing you're not riding one of your bikes either."

"Right," she said. "Today, it's my Aston Martin red convertible—with the top down."

Bryan explained that it would be Mariko's job to find the girl and bring her home, which meant heading for Manchester.

"Once I get there, who do I start with?" asked Mariko.

"With a real piece of shit," said Bryan. "Tom Lewis. He's a deputy—works at the jail. He denied even seeing the girl, but we hacked their security system and have him on video. She was there, and he spent a lot of time talking to her. All indications are that he must have arranged for someone to spirit her away."

"You mean like kidnapped?" asked Mariko.

"We don't know for sure," said Bryan. She could have been taken against her will or someone could have talked her into going with them. What we do know is that we haven't heard from her—or, I should say, her mother hasn't heard from her. We also can't locate her cell phone. There's a good chance the phone is no longer in her possession. At one point in the video, we see her give her phone to this Lewis character. We don't know for what purpose. We don't know if Lewis kept the phone or gave it back."

The strain of the hours without sleep was taking a toll on Bryan's voice. His throat was extremely dry, his body felt heavy, and he was having trouble holding anything without shaking. He discreetly popped another pill, took a long drink of water, cleared his throat, and continued—hoping no one noticed.

"Getting the girl home is *paramount*," said Bryan. "But keep the pain clinics on your radar. I want to know what's going on with them. They might have something to do with the girl or the missing husband. I don't know, but involved or not, if they are pill mills, we need to do what we can to close them down. Finally, stay alert—if you smell anything related to Sam's terrorist business, call home. Call home fast."

Mariko spoke to Sam on the display. "I could use a little clarification on this," she said. "Do I need to report anyone who looks Middle Eastern?"

"Not unless there is something about them that sets off your alarm bells," said Sam. "I appreciate what Bryan said to you, but I know you guys will err on the right side—so let your gut guide you. On the other hand, a large group of young Middle Eastern men is a no brainer. We need to know ASAP! Even if they look harmless, regard them as dangerous suspects. However, you shouldn't take any action other than reporting back immediately. If they are who we are looking for, just making eye contact could put you at significant risk. Okay?"

"Thanks, Sam," said Mariko. "That helps."

Sam nodded and added, "Even without the terrorist issue, Mariko, you need to be careful while you're looking for the girl. There are so many angles here. She could be in the hands of traffickers. There are bad apples in local police. Then there are the clinics. There is money involved in every facet—*big* money—and big money usually means dangerous people. So, stay on your toes. I don't want anything to happen to any of you."

"Thanks for the warning, Sam," said Mariko. "We will."

"Sam's right," Bryan added. "While you should try to stay out of harm's way, you should also carry personal protection in case you find yourself in trouble. I want you armed and able to defend yourselves."

"I wouldn't think of leaving home without a firearm of some kind," said Mariko. "I'm carrying something new—a four-barrel 38 from Signal 9 Defense out in Gallatin. They're not shipping it yet so mine is a prerelease model. They want my feedback."

Her colleagues looked impressed. Mariko indulged them.

"So far it's fantastic," said Mariko. "You know the problem with an automatic—they jam when you need them most."

The men around the table and on the screen nodding knowingly.

"But the Reliant is just four barrels in a breakaway configuration—like a shotgun," she continued. "There's nothing to jam. Plus, it's a big punch in a little package—less than six inches long; weighs in at only a pound fully loaded. My wardrobe doesn't always make concealment easy, you know."

Again, the men nodded in unison.

"So much for the commercial," Bryan said with a grin. "What about you, Tony?"

Mariko interrupted, "Sorry, Bryan. It's just that I'm not easily impressed. The Reliant impressed me enough that I wanted you guys to know about it. If you have ever faced the wrong end of a 1911 while you are holding a jammed weapon, you know what I mean."

"Enough chitchat, guys," Bryan said. "We need to go to work."

"You know my preference," said Tony. "I have my tactical baton and, so far, it's kept me safe enough."

"I'd feel better if you added a weapon with a little more standoff reach," said Bryan. "I want you to take this with you."

Bryan handed Tony a tiny revolver.

"It's from North American Arm—a five-shot miniature. The revolver fires a 22-magnum shell. Put it in your pocket just in case, okay?"

Tony chuckled. "Sure thing—but I'll have to keep it concealed because it sure as hell isn't going to scare anyone."

"It might not, Tony, but it'll kill someone."

"Roger that, Bryan!"

"One more item before I let you loose," said Bryan. "I have the latest satellite communicator for each of you. The new Aurora system is always on. Press the red Talk button to connect to me as the control. Select the blue button to automatically connect to the entire case team—that's the three of you—Tony, Mariko, and you, too, Sam—plus the boss once he's back on his feet. Sam, your unit is being delivered. It should be there within the hour."

"No offense, Bryan, but the last thing I need is another piece of hardware to haul around," said Sam.

"I second that," said Mariko. "This skinny suit doesn't leave much room for more carry-alongs. Remember, I'm already carrying the Reliant."

"There are three different variations in the boxset I'm giving you," said Bryan. "The pocket version is no bigger than a pen drive. It's only two inches long and half an inch wide. if you prefer, there's a watch version you can wear on your wrist, or a pendent version with a chain to go around the neck. Aurora could save your life, so make one the three variations work, okay?"

"You're the boss," said Mariko, "but it is going to put a wrinkle in my pants."

"So, wear the damn thing on your wrist!" Bryan said before turning to Sam.

"I hope you won't have a problem with this unit either," he continued. "It works on the L-band to a G2 geosynchronous satellite. That means the signal always gets through—no drops, no lost calls, no dead spots. It's new, like Mariko's handgun. The Aurora is not yet released commercially. It's way ahead of anything you guys have in the FBI or Homeland Security. This is a chance to see it in action because you're going to want it for your organization."

"It will go in the pocket with my change," said Sam.

"Any questions?" asked Bryan. "Okay, then. Mariko and Tony, you have your marching orders—get out of here and go to work. Sam, I need you to stay with me for a minute longer."

Chapter 25

Top Secret Weapon

Bryan was now alone in the case room, except for the screen image of Sam Littleton delivered through a secure satellite connection. He needed to discuss some things with Sam in private.

"I know you have your hands full with the terrorist alert," said Bryan, "but there are two things I need from you. If possible, let's find out what really happened to the first husband. If the doctor offed himself intentionally or otherwise, okay? But if not, then we have a murderer running around on our playing board—right in the middle of this other stuff we're dealing with, the girl and the missing husband. If it's murder, he or she will strike again. The next time, we could lose a player—one of us or the wife, daughter, or husband number two, if he isn't already dead."

"I can put some of my DEA people on it," said Sam. "Using Drug Enforcement won't take away resources from dealing with threats of terror. We know there were drugs involved, so using DEA isn't much of a leap."

"Thanks, Sam. You know our Big John, John Felts. He can bring your people up-to-date. John has been looking at the first husband's death. He checked with the people in Metro's Major Crimes Unit. In turn, they've been in touch with the Boston authorities. All four hundred pounds of Felts comes down on the side of foul play. As far as he and his friends are concerned, the suicide angle just doesn't pass the smell test."

"We've worked with Felts before and I trust his instincts," said Sam.

"Fantastic. Now for the second thing," said Bryan. "I hear that you guys have a piece of software, code named Locard. I understand that it is a breakthrough in artificial intelligence software—something people are calling 'digital reasoning.'"

Sam shifted in his seat. He held up his hand and said, "Just hold that; I'll be back."

Littleton got up from his chair and disappeared from the display screen. Bryan looked at his watch. Just as he was beginning to wonder if their meeting was over, Littleton was back.

"I needed to make sure the room on this end was secure," said Sam. Before we go any further with this discussion, I need you to do the same."

The high-tech conference table in the case room included an embedded touchscreen display. Bryan was quickly able to engage the locks on all physical access points in or out of the room and electrically closed the light- and soundproof window shutters. He disengaged cameras and audio devices that might be hackable and dropped all Internet, cell, and dish connections except the secure feed connecting Sam to the room. He engaged the room's covert sound option—rushing water—and activated a ceiling-mounted microburst laser system that caused minute fluctuations in the temperature of exterior windows and walls to counter any attempt to recreate sound waves from glass or wall material movement in harmony with the human voice.

"Okay, Sam, we're now super secure. Nothing in or out. It's just the two of us."

"I don't know where you get your information," said Sam, "but you simply knowing about Locard means someone is risking a jail term. Locard is drop-dead top secret. You shouldn't know about it, and the two of us sure as hell shouldn't be talking about it."

"Just hear me out, Sam. There's nothing sinister going on here. No one needs to go to jail. We know about it because we've been working along on the same lines. Our people, mine and yours, live in the same work and knowledge circle. My people and your people do the same research. You can't stop the information bleed when people are working so closely on the same things, dealing with the same resources and concepts."

"Just the same, this makes me nervous," said Sam.

"In this case, our work and yours follows Edmond Locard's exchange principle," said Sam. "I assume that's the reason your people gave this software the Locard code name. But that told us everything."

Bryan's team had, in fact, been building on Locard's exchange principle, the notion that a perpetrator of a crime will always bring something into the crime scene and they will always leave with something from it. In simple terms, *every contact leaves a trace*. As mentioned earlier, at the WHC brain trust, Bryan called these traces "breadcrumbs."

"We use those breadcrumbs to find people," he said. "My understanding is that your digital reasoning software goes even further. It has the capability to predict the future when the pattern or breadcrumbs change. In other words, it can anticipate that 'something is up'—*and* take the last step of estimating what that something is, and when and where it will happen."

Sam sat for a few seconds in silence, choosing his words carefully.

"You've got it," he finally said. "Provided you have the considerable training and experience needed to work with it. The more we use it, the better Locard becomes. The software genius who developed it says that it gets smarter. It becomes more predictive. For example, if we identified one person as an assassin, then someone else we are tracking, and Mr. A starts talking to Mr. B who then communicates to the assassin, we might predict based on other factors that A is planning to do harm to someone."

Bryan nodded. He understood completely.

"If you add to that the software's ability to read and understand human communication in context," continued Sam, "we can often predict who the assassin's target is. People don't say *I want you to kill person C*. They might say *I have a house I want you to paint*. Well, the software has learned that painting a house is shoptalk for a hit. A communication may describe the target in an agreed-upon code. *Paint the house on 4th Street.* The software can work backward to find possibilities for 4th Street by scanning digital data connected to all contact points—points of contact not only between A, B, C and the assassin, but all the contacts of A, B, C and the assassin to others and all their contacts, etc. Locard can search worldwide—everything including voice, text, and other digital objects. We are talking about everything on the Web or on the internal systems of individuals, companies, governments, and other entities. If it's connected to the Web, Locard can access it. Locard can go as deep and for as long as we let it go. It does that continually. It's like that leaf idea with family tree software. When Locard spots a possible piece of the puzzle we are trying to solve, it gives us a leaf and it keeps on trucking. Since we got our hands on Locard, we have stopped more than a thousand active terror and criminal plots. We were able to close them down *before* they became operational."

Bryan could hardly wait for Sam to finish.

"I want it!" he said. "No, it is more than that. I *must* have it. You have to give it to me!"

"Bryan, are you crazy? I can't give it to you. This is the digital equivalent of the atomic bomb. In fact, now that I know you know about it, I should kill you! I'm joking, of course, but the point is we don't want the bad guys to know we have this capability, and we sure as hell don't want to risk it ever falling into their hands."

Bryan persisted.

"Think about it for a minute," he said. "How often do you guys—FBI, CIA, and Homeland Security—come to us because Congress or the courts have limited what you can do? If the do-gooders and politically correct advocates get a hint of what you just described to me, they will shut you down in a flash. The courts would never give you a warrant to cast your net that wide. You know it. That's why you must keep this secret—to keep it hidden from the people who would shut it down. If this intelligence capability is important, you must give it to us. You don't have a choice. If you don't give it to us and they shut you down—and they will—you won't be able to move the software to a contractor like us without going to jail. I mean, you're talking about predicting terrorists' acts and crimes before they happen. You know that under our laws, as an agency of the government, you can't do that! You have to wait until there has been a crime before you can act. We don't have to play by those rules."

Sam paused again, thinking carefully about how to continue.

"No one is going to give me permission for what you are asking," he said. "It's not in the cards. You know that!"

"When did permission ever stop you from doing what you knew was right?" asked Bryan. "If you don't get this into friendly hands outside of the government, this exceptional country that the world depends on for the preservation of freedom will lose the best tool it has ever had in its fight against evil."

Sam said nothing, but Bryan knew he would not let the world down. He would do what had to be done.

Finally, Sam said, "It's a strange thing to have to come to grips with the idea that a private group of patriots, hidden among so many beautiful women at the WHC, is a more secure and safe place for this software than with our own government. But, I know you're right. At least for now—for today. None of us know what the future holds. I must make decisions for the world as I know it to be right now. And I will, Bryan. We'll get together soon."

Sam disconnected and the case room fell silent.

Chapter 26

Mark Rollins Opens His Eyes

I opened my eyes to a scene I knew too well. I raised my hand to rub the sleep from my eyes and saw that I was connected to old friends—IVs and monitoring devices. The clear liquid was probably just to keep me hydrated and the white stuff, I remembered, was the bag that they called "steak and potatoes." *They've been feeding me*, I thought. *Intravenously dripping nourishment into my veins.* I turned my head toward the window. Next to it I saw my wife, Sarah, curled up in a leather armchair—*probably a recliner*, I thought. *I wonder why she hasn't reclined.*

At first I tried to think. *Why am I back in a hospital?* My back hurt. I looked for the bed's control and my hand found it. *It's like riding a bike,* I thought. *Once you learn to work these beds—you don't forget.* I raised the bed into a sitting position. Sarah stirred.

"Mark, you're awake!" she said.

I could see she was relieved. I asked her why I was there.

"You were in a car accident," she said. "Don't you remember?"

Instantly, I thought of Tony.

"Tony? Is he all right?" I asked.

"Yes, don't worry," said Sarah. "He has a broken arm, a couple of cracked ribs, and lots of bruises, but nothing serious. They've already released him."

"Thank goodness. How long have I been here?"

"This is day four."

I could hardly believe it.

"No kidding," said Sarah. "They had to operate."

"Where? Give me the rundown. Do I have all my body parts?"

I winked at my wife.

"Externally you do—nothing missing," she chided. "You had a nasty bump on your head, but the worst was an abdominal injury—a piece of metal penetrated your abdomen. You lost a lot of blood, and they were very afraid of infection."

"Who did the surgery?"

"Dr. Porter."

"I guess that's good—a return visit," I said. "By now he knows his way around down there. Maybe he should just install a zipper so he doesn't have to keep cutting me open."

I was putting up a good front, but Sarah could tell I was trying to feel my abdomen, hoping I wouldn't find an ostomy bag. Thankfully, I didn't.

"So, they were able to put everything back together?" I asked.

"Yes. They reconnected the pipes. You have a little less colon and a couple of quarts of new blood. All in all, the doc says you were lucky—lucky to come out of this alive. Another fifteen minutes and you might not have been."

"Whose blood did I get?" I asked, suddenly curious.

"Mine, of course. Remember? I'm Type O negative—a universal donor."

"Yes, but I worry about you," I said. "What happens when you need blood? Who else do we know with your same Type O?"

"That is chasing after windmills, my love," she said gently. "It isn't something we need to worry about right now. Right now, you need to get well. You have a lot of people to thank for being alive."

"Doc Porter and you. Who else?"

"Number one on your list should be Sam Littleton. He got you out of there within minutes of the explosion. There was a fire, and you were about to be barbecued."

"I'm beginning to remember," I said. "There was an explosion and then we were rammed by a truck."

"Yes, a Greyhound bus and a propane truck collided. The bus was empty except for the driver, thank goodness. The propane exploded. You and Tony were two of the lucky ones."

"So, it was just an accident?" I asked, remembering suddenly that Sam had been trying to convey some intel right before impact.

"Yes," said Sarah. "You mean you thought it might have been intentional—like a terrorist attack?"

"Sam Littleton had just called me when everything exploded. I remember he said something was going on in the city and he wanted my help. I thought the explosion might have been related."

"Sam has been here every day checking on you. He hasn't indicated that it was anything other than an accident. I did read where they arrested someone who they think was planning a Boston Marathon-style bomb attack on Bonnaroo—pressure cooker bombs. They say he was a lone wolf, not part of an organized plot. Maybe that's what Sam was calling you about."

"Yeah . . . doesn't matter now," I said. "Where is the doctor?"

"Are you in pain?"

"Yes, a little, but mainly I want to find out when I can get out of here. Speaking of here, where am I?"

"You're in Centennial," said Sarah. "Your surgeon had you transferred here yesterday from Vanderbilt."

"Is Glenda Adams still a patient here?"

"That's the woman with the missing daughter you've been trying to help?"

"Yes," I said quickly. "Is she still here?"

"I don't know. Tony has been filling in for you with her. I'm sure that he or Bryan will be here tonight and can bring you up-to-date. Right now, why don't you put that bed back down and rest?"

I felt lightheaded and tired—very tired. Just the act of sitting up and talking with Sarah had drained my strength. I realized that I must have been seriously hurt. It hadn't been just a bump on the head or a little scratch. I shut my eyes and could see the crash all over again. Then I felt the stabbing pain. I jerked my eyes open to break the spell. I looked at Sarah and said, "Yeah, I think I might just need to do that. Then I need to talk to her."

"Who?" she asked.

"Glenda Adams."

Chapter 27

Glenda Returns Home

Glenda was out of the hospital. The doctor told her that her body would not accept the chemo any longer. There was nothing else they could do for her. They suggested hospice, explaining that the pain was going to get worse. She would eventually have to have heavy doses of morphine. The pain was already rough. With morphine, she could sleep to the end. Right now, that didn't seem too bad, but it would have to wait. Before she could sleep, she had to get Sammie back while she still could. She would deal with the pain without the morphine.

When Mark Rollins awoke the second time, he called her room before she had left the hospital. He told her that he suspected one of the guards at the jail, Tom Lewis, had either taken Sammie or arranged for someone else to take her.

Glenda wasn't going to wait. That man was going to tell her where she could find Sammie.

She had taken a taxi to her house where she planned to get her gun, a Taurus 451 revolver that had belonged to her second husband. The weapon was designed for concealed carry with a two-and-a-half-inch barrel. The barrel length didn't matter. She knew she didn't need to be a marksman—not with that gun. It chambered 410 shotgun shells. All she had to do was get close—make sure the little red dot shined on the man's midsection. Then pull the trigger.

He's just a piece of shit anyway, she thought. *If I kill him—and I probably will—the world will be a better place.*

Glenda hadn't laughed in a long time, but the thought made her chuckle.

What would they do to me anyway, she asked herself. *Arrest me? Put me on trial? Execute me? No!* she thought, a new logic taking hold. *God has given me cancer for a reason—I can rid the earth of any lowlife I want. They can't punish me. I will be dead and gone before a trial. God fixed it so the rules don't apply to me. They haven't since I learned about the cancer. I don't want Sammie to have to deal with the same lowlifes I've put up with, and now I don't have to.*

Every few minutes a terrible cramp crumpled Glenda. Each took her breath away. She clamped her eyes shut and clenched her teeth until it passed. Normally the cramps would have made driving impossible. But, now was different. She had to get to Sammie, and that meant she had to drive no matter what. Despite the pain. Despite the cramps. She would get it done! The car keys were in a basket on the small chest in the front foyer where she had left them the last time she had driven. She grabbed the keys and started for the kitchen and the door to the garage.

Glenda froze. She heard something at the back door. She could see the knob turn as someone tried to open the locked handle. *How did they get in the garage?* she thought. She crept closer to the door and listened. She heard whoever it was trying to unlock the door. *Did they have a key?* She looked to make sure the deadbolt was engaged. It was. *The pantry—I could hide in the pantry.*

The previous owners called the space a butler's pantry. It was unusually large. She opened the door, hoping it wouldn't squeak. Sometimes it did, sometimes not. This time it remained silent. She pulled the door closed but didn't completely shut it. She had the pistol in her hand and watched through the small crack she had left by leaving the door unlatched. Now it sounded like the intruder was using an electric device of some kind. She could see the door into the garage. She watched the toggle in the handle of the lock move to the unlocked position. The intruder tried the knob and realized that the deadbolt was still locked. In her mind's eye, she knew he was starting to work on the deadbolt. She heard the drill sound again. It took only a few more seconds before she saw the deadbolt move. It was unlocked; the door opened.

For a few seconds, nothing happened. No one entered. *The alarm. They were waiting and listening for an alarm.* There was none, only silence. A man entered the house.

Who the hell is he? Glenda's thought frantically. *I have my phone. Why don't I call 911? It's too late now! He would hear if I called now.*

The man just stood in the kitchen—*listening*. Glenda's heart was racing. She tried to breathe quietly. She was afraid that if she even shifted her weight, he would hear her. *Can he smell me?* She tried to think. *Did I wear any perfume today?* Then another thought made her panic. *The phone—what if someone calls or I get a message?* She took out the phone and began fumbling with the two objects, the phone and the pistol. She managed to move the switch on the side of the phone to airplane mode.

The man shouted, "Hello! Is anyone here?" He listened and then he did it again. "Hello? Is anyone here?" Satisfied that he was alone, he went back out the door and returned in a few minutes carrying something heavy. He set it down. Shut the door. Picked it up and walked out of the kitchen.

Glenda's mind was spinning. *Should I run? He might have someone helping him—outside or in the garage.* She shifted her weight and tried to think. The cramp hit her and it took all her resolve to hold the scream in. *I can't stay like this much longer,* she thought. The pain subsided, and her eyes cleared. *What was the thing he brought? A propane tank? Why would he bring that into the house?*

Twenty minutes of wondering and waiting had passed when it hit her. *He's going to burn down my house.*

The man was now in the dining room. She could hear him; he was on the phone.

"Yeah, the place is empty," he said. "She's still in the hospital. I got it under control. I told you I would take care of it. I checked. There's a basement, and I set the bomb up in there. When we know the old lady and brat are here, we can detonate it with a phone call. The place will go up like a rocket."

There was a pause. Glenda held her breath.

"No, no; it will be right next to the furnace. No one will suspect a thing. It will just be one of those unfortunate explosions from an old faulty furnace that leaked gas. Plus, an old propane tank stored nearby." He laughed. "They tell people not to do that all the time, don't they? But the peeps still do it, and look what happens."

There was silence for a minute. The man listened to whoever was on the other end.

"Damn it, sis, I said I would handle this. It will be done and there won't be anything or anybody left to connect us with this shit."

She heard the man moving. He had ended his call. She pushed the numbers on the phone screen: 911. Whispered the words and her address. Then put the phone in her pocket and tightened her grip on her revolver. She stepped out of the pantry. Shined the little red dot on the shocked man's middle—and fired.

Chapter 28

Tony's Crime Scene

"Thanks for the heads-up, Bryan," Tony said. "There are cops all over the place, and they don't look very friendly. I don't know how they would have reacted if I had tried to pull into the drive without stopping. I parked down the road a bit. If you still want me inside the house, you're going to have to pull some strings to get me in there."

"The Adams house is on Del Rio Pike within the city limits so I assume the cops you mentioned are Franklin police, right?" asked Bryan. "I had the system set to monitor any traffic related to names and addresses involved so the report of the 911 call flashed on one of my displays. That's when I buzzed you."

"Well, the Franklin City troops are part of the cavalry, but it looks like everyone else is here too—Brentwood, Nashville, and state troopers. Looks like a police convention."

"A call for backup went out to the surrounding areas because of the unknowns involved," said Bryan. "But, if this does turn out to be a serious crime scene, the investigation will default to the TBI. The bureau director is a friend of ours. I'll call him and get you in. Standby."

Tony sat tight for ten minutes, then fifteen, before his phone buzzed. Bryan had worked his magic. Tony was in.

"They have me fully suited up," Tony said as he entered the house. Bryan was on the line. "TBI jacket, overalls, gloves, and booties. Still, they made it clear I observe only. I'm in the entrance hall facing what seems to be a kitchen and den. There is blood everywhere. They haven't found any bodies, but with all this blood, there has to be one somewhere. I've been paired with Special Agent Ed Poe. He tells me that there's also a blood trail leading from the kitchen through the garage. It stops in the driveway. Whoever was bleeding must have gotten into a car. They either drove or were driven away. Investigators won't let me in the kitchen or the garage—afraid I'll contaminate their crime scene. Poe tells me they have bloody footprints of a second person. Someone other than the bleeder, someone who stepped in some of the blood and left a trail from the kitchen into the garage. Poe says there is no car currently in the garage, but there is evidence that there had been one. They speculate that the second person got into that parked car and drove away. Between me and you, pal, I would assume that second person is Glenda Adams. And Bryan, if she is the cause of all this blood, I don't want to get on her bad side."

"It could also have been the missing husband," Bryan said.

"If it was, he has very small feet," said Tony. "The footprint was small—more likely a woman's, according to Agent Poe. On the other hand, we're sure that the bleeder was a male. There is so much blood that we have the bleeder's own tracks where he went out the garage's pedestrian door, and even a couple of partials in the driveway before he probably got into a car. Given the size of those footprints, the bleeder was definitely a male."

Bryan asked, "If person number two was Mrs. Adams, who was the bleeder and what happened to him?"

"The only male on our radar is the missing husband," said Tony. "Until we have something else, that's my working assumption—the husband is the bleeder. As for what happened to him in that house, my hypothesis is that he was shot by our second person—aka Glenda Adams. Odds are she took the weapon with her when she left. Which brings up some interesting questions."

"Which are?" asked Bryan.

Tony launched into his list. "Why? What's next? Why did she shoot the bleeder? I think the more dangerous questions are her location, her destination, and what she's planning to do next."

"Maybe she's just confused," offered Bryan. "Scared, running away from whatever the bleeder was up to."

"I don't buy that, Bryan. It doesn't feel that way to me. She left without waiting for people to show up in response to her 911 call. She had to have a reason for leaving. I think she's going after someone."

"Are they going to let you do what we sent you there for?" asked Bryan. "To go through the place and look for things that might give you a clue as to the whereabouts of the husband?"

"Not a chance," said Tony, "but if you're looking for the husband, I repeat—start with the hospitals or the morgue. Because if he is the bleeder, he's not going to last long without medical attention. And, Bryan, one more thing."

"What's that?"

"You need to give Mariko a heads-up on this. That Adams woman—if it is her, and it looks like it is—has a gun, and she may be on a campaign of some kind. I figure there are two possibilities. First, she might be trying to finish off the bleeder who we assume is husband number two. Or second, and I think more likely, she is headed for Manchester to find her daughter. That might put her on the same track as Mariko's."

Tony suddenly stopped talking. Bryan could hear commotion in the background, then yelling.

"Something's happening!" yelled Tony in a frantic voice.

Bryan could hear him fumbling with his phone.

"They found a bomb in the basement!" said Tony. "Everyone's out, lab guys, photographer—everyone! We've got to get out of the house."

Chapter 29

Life or Death Call

"Who is this?" Dr. Mick asked. "My nurse said you told her it was a matter of life or death?"

"Goddamn right it is!" said Tom Lewis, the moonlighting guard Carlos had hired to drive him to the Franklin address. "Maybe yours, Doc. I've got the boss man in the car—he's been shot. He's bleeding out, man. You got to do something!"

"Take him to the hospital."

"Are you crazy?" said Tom. "I said he's been shot. I can't take him to no damn hospital. I'm coming to you. That's why I called. If the cops don't get me for speeding, I'll be there in twenty minutes max. If I were you, I would get ready for him because I'm going to dump him in your lap and run! I don't want anything more to do with this shit."

"You can't do that."

"The hell I can't," said Tom. "Watch me! All I was supposed to do was drive him somewhere. I don't know anything. All I get is a few bucks for playing guard. You're the ones selling drugs to people. This is your business, not mine. What I got is an important-ass dude that may be dying from God knows who shot him or why, and I gotta get rid of him. That's what I'm going to do. Get rid of him on your doorstep. You want to take him to the hospital after that, I don't give a shit."

"Okay then," said Dr. Mick. "Bring him to me."

After disconnecting from the call, Dr. Mick took several deep breaths as he tried to think through the problem. He looked at his watch—2:15 p.m. There was still a line of people waiting to get into the clinic. He needed to get rid of them. The clinic interior arrangement was standard for a medical office. A separate reception and waiting area. A door leading to the examining rooms. Through that door, there was a nurse's station. Most of the time there were two women behind the counter. The doctor called them his assistants. Today there were three on duty. They were neither trained nurses nor nurse practitioners—just attractive young girls he employed to play the role. Beyond the nurses were three examining rooms where the doctor met with patients.

Dr. Mick came out of the third exam room, which also doubled as his office. He spoke to his three assistants.

"I need to close early today," he said quickly. "Grace, start telling our clients that the doctor has been called away on a medical emergency. Emma, you can go home as soon as we lock up."

The oldest of the three assistants was Connie Maynord. Trained or not, she wouldn't be afraid if he needed help with the wounded man.

"Connie, I may need your help with a special patient. There will be something extra in it for you, so stick around."

Grace stepped outside on the entrance ramp and made the announcement. They had done this before—closed early by pinning a preprinted sign on the door—*Closed for the remainder of the day.* There were unhappy people in the unserved line, but the guard saw to it that those wanting to see the doctor vacated the premises. Grace and Emma worked at Walmart before the doctor charmed them into working for him. The money was great. Both were making almost three times what Walmart paid. Both asked no questions and were happy to get off early. Connie was different; the doctor had brought her with him from Florida.

With the door locked, the staff gone except for Connie, and the parking area empty, Dr. Mick made the call he didn't want to make. It was the name and number he was told to call if things got bad. And the shit had just hit the fan.

— ƒ —

The woman on the end of the line identified herself as Lena De La Cruz.

"All right, Doc," she snapped. "This had better be important."

Dr. Mick spoke quickly. "One of the hired help called. Tom Lewis from the sheriff's. He said he has Carlos with him and is bringing him to the clinic. Lewis said your brother has been shot. From what he told me, it may be bad. I'm not really equipped to handle trauma cases. What do you want me to do?"

Lena didn't answer immediately. Two completely different, even contrary, issues were fighting for control of her thoughts. Both dealt with survival. *Why was he shot? Would it lead back to her? What about the heart and lungs? No matter what, they must live! No matter what happens to Carlos—I need his heart and his lungs!*

"Doc, let me make this clear," she said. "Under no circumstance are you to let Carlos's body die. Save him if you can, but if you can't, keep this body alive until we can harvest his organs."

"I don't understand," said Dr. Mick.

"Okay, maybe this will get through to you, Doc. Do what I tell you and I'll make you a rich man. If you lose the heart and lungs, I will have you killed. Do you understand me now?"

Dr. Mick thought for a few seconds. He didn't understand much, but he understood rich, and he understood killed.

"What do you mean, rich?" he asked.

"Two million," said Lena without hesitating.

"Well off, but not rich—rich starts at ten million."

"Okay. Ten million dollars," she hissed, "but *only* if you save the heart and the lungs. Tell me what you need, and I'll get it to you."

"You mean for a transplant?"

"I mean do what the hell you have to do to keep his friggin' heart and lungs alive. Yes, for a transplant, goddammit—a transplant to be performed by someone else. Somebody who has done it a thousand times. All you have to do is keep the organs viable."

"Okay. As soon as I see your brother, I'll call," said Dr. Mick. "If it's as bad as it sounds, we'll need to get him on life support equipment ASAP!"

"Do you have that at the clinic?"

"Hell, no," he snapped. "All I do is sign scripts."

"If I get the equipment to the clinic, can you operate it?"

"Yes. But you need to get it here fast!"

"I will have it there," said Lena. "You just keep him alive."

After the call ended, the doctor smiled and worried at the same time. Ten million was a lot of money. Maybe too much money. It might be incentive enough to get him killed.

Suddenly, Tom Lewis pounded desperately on the door to the clinic.

Chapter 30

Sherlock, aka Locard

Bryan felt almost giddy when he made the secure call to tell Sam that his copy of Locard was up and running.

"If it makes you any happier," said Bryan, "around here it's called Sherlock. We tinkered around the edges, removed the original coder tags, and tried our best to build a case that Sherlock and Locard are not the same piece of software."

"Thanks, Bryan," said Sam. "I just hope it's enough to keep me out of the pen."

"We've only just started with Sherlock," Bryan continued. "Even though the prior activity metadata stream you segregated out for us is limited, we're getting some early results. Are you aware of the scene at Glenda Adams's residence?"

"Of course," said Sam. "I understand why you would be interested—no, concerned—about that mess. It must be tied to your case of the missing girl. For us, however, it doesn't appear related to our terrorist concern. It's off our radar."

"You're right about what it means to us," said Bryan. "But I don't think you can ignore this. Granted it may or may not have anything to do with terrorist activity, but, at a minimum, it has everything to do with the diversion of legal drugs for illegal purposes. That's just as much up your alley as terrorism. And it's possible we've stumbled on a connection involving both—the girl and the terrorist thing."

"I'm listening," said Sam.

"Since Manchester is so relevant to both the missing girl and your terrorism concern, we set Sherlock to track any out-of-pattern event in the area," said Bryan. "In other words, any new event—an occurrence that wasn't a repeat of prior activity. We picked up a flight plan for a private jet flying from Miami to the Tullahoma Regional Airport. That facility is only fifteen miles from the pill mill in Manchester that Rollins and Tony identified. The plane is owned by the same corporate group that owns the clinic. The president of that corporation, Lena De La Cruz, just happened to receive a phone call shortly before takeoff from a cell phone located in the Manchester area."

Bryan sounded excited. The software was working and the case was progressing.

"That wouldn't be particularly meaningful except for the mega tags included in the captured digital stream," he continued. "*Shot, bleeding,* and *drugs*. The outgoing call to De La Cruz was from the personal cell of the clinic's doctor. Tracking back from there, that call was preceded by an incoming call to the clinic's main phone from a cell phone belonging to Tom Lewis. He's the local sheriff's employee that Rollins suspects was involved in the disappearance of Glenda Adams's daughter. Again, the words *shot* and *blood* were tagged. But Sherlock wasn't done. Working with the tags *De La Cruz, shot, blood, drugs,* and a few others, Sherlock identified an earlier call from one Carlos De La Cruz to Lewis. The metadata stream included an address. Do you want to know the address?"

"Let me guess," said Sam. "The location of our suspected shooting—Mrs. Adams's home address."

"You nailed it!" shouted Bryan. "Sherlock also identified Lena and Carlos De La Cruz as twins and the kingpins behind a widespread illegal drug enterprise disguised as legitimate pain management clinics."

"So, whatever unfolded at the Adams home is directly connected to both the disappearance of the girl and the pill mills," said Sam.

"That's right," said Bryan. "But I'd be remiss if I didn't point out that that plane is landing in proximity to the Arnold wind tunnels. That may be a coincidence, but you can't discount the connection between the illegal drugs business and terrorism. One generates lots of cash and the other needs lots of cash to fund operations."

"That's a stretch," said Sam. "But to be safe, we'll deploy some folks in that direction. Let me know if you come up with anything more."

"Will do," said Bryan. "We're just getting started with Sherlock, but the software looks like it could easily get away from us—drown us in information. This thing has serious power."

"Yes, that's been Locard's biggest problem," said Sam. "You can literally be blinded—unable to see the forest for the trees."

Chapter 31

Glenda Goes Hunting

Through dazed, glassy eyes, Glenda stared at the deputy manning the information desk. "I'm looking for someone," she said.

Her jacket covered the bloodstain on her blouse. She didn't know if the shooting had been discovered yet. She had hung up on 911 but knew they would have responded anyway. She also had no idea who she had shot. He was just a silhouette, but somehow she knew it wasn't Tom Lewis. That's why she was here.

"If you tell me the name, I can look him or her up on the computer and give you a status," the deputy said. "Was it someone arrested today?"

"Arrested?" said Glenda. "No, he works here. Lewis—Tom Lewis."

"Yes, ma'am, but he is not on duty right now. Got no idea when he will be in so why don't you tell me what you want?"

Glenda's adrenal glands were pulsing. Her metabolism was rocketing, readying her body for fight or flight. Her glassy eyes were now hardened, piercing. "No," she said sternly. "

"I'm Tom's nephew," the man said. "If it's family business, you can tell me."

"No!" she shouted abruptly. "This is just for him. Where can I find him?"

"Lady, you know I can't give you that information. You're just going to have to tell me your name and phone number. When he comes on duty, I'll tell him you want him to call you."

"When is that?" she snapped.

"When is what?"

"You said he would be coming on duty," said Glenda. "When is that?"

"Ma'am, what is your name?"

"I'll wait for him," she said. "I see his name on that desk. I'll wait for him there."

"Ma'am, I'm afraid I can't let you do that. If you want to wait in the visitors' area, that's your call. Civilians are not allowed on the other side of that barrier."

Glenda was fuming. "Look, mister, I'm tired of this shit. Why don't you just tell me when the hell he'll be coming on duty?"

Tom's nephew tried to remain firm, but he felt the situation escalating, could sense this woman was on the verge of . . . something. Exactly what, he couldn't be sure. "Ma'am, until you tell me your business with Tom, we're done here! Either take a seat in the visitors' area or leave. There are other people here who need my assistance."

The sheriff's information officer failed to notice the shift in the woman's body language. If he had, he might have realized the futility in telling her to sit or leave. Glenda was determined. She wasn't going to sit and she wasn't going leave. But, she had decided not to push the information officer any further. She desperately wanted to get to Tom Lewis's desk. Sammie would have called if she had had her phone. Lewis probably took it from her. It had a pink cover and Sammie had written her initials on the back with a black Sharpie. Glenda wanted to search Lewis's desk. If he took it, it might be there—in his desk, which was just on the other side of the low wall that separated the visitors' area from the rest of the room. The front of Lewis's desk was pushed against the wall. If she stood on her toes, leaned over, and really stretched hard, she could reach the top of the desk, but not the drawers. She needed to get closer to get inside.

— ƒ —

Tom Lewis was badly shaken. After dropping the wounded man off at the clinic, he hurried to his trailer and changed clothes. He was sure there were still traces of blood on him, but he was already late to clock in and he just couldn't handle a cold shower with the water hose. His discarded clothes were bloody. He decided to burn them in the steel drum in his backyard where he burned trash. He threw the clothes in the drum and doused them in coal oil. He found a piece of cardboard, ignited it, and threw the burning cardboard into the drum. Still shaking, he got in his car and headed for the jail.

Glenda waited. She waited for a chance to get to Lewis's desk, and she was hunting for Lewis. There was no other plan. She was on autopilot. She was going to find Sammie and she knew Lewis was the first step. She watched the information officer, who picked up the phone and called someone. After a few minutes, a second officer walked up to the information desk where Tom Lewis's nephew mouthed the words *Be right back*. He headed for the men's restroom. While the substitute sat at the desk, Glenda rose from her seat just as an elderly woman and her husband came in the door. The woman was crying, clearly upset. The newcomers immediately went to the information desk and started talking to the substitute. It was Glenda's chance. She knew it and she took it. She quickly closed the short distance between her seat in the visitors' area and the low wall. She went through the free swing gate to Lewis's desk. She didn't need to go any further than the first drawer. There was the pink iPhone; it had to be Sammie's. She snatched it, went back through the gate, and headed for the front door. As she was leaving the gated area, Lewis's nephew stepped out of the restroom.

"Lady!" he shouted. "What were you doing?"

She didn't stop or slow down. She didn't acknowledge him. He was after her, fast.

"Lady, stop where you are!"

She kept going just as the substitute guard called to Tom's nephew, "Hey, man, don't leave. I need your help over here."

The deputy stopped, then turned back. "Okay, I'm coming. Don't have a cow." He watched Glenda escape out the door and whispered, "Crazy bitch!"

Glenda ran down the steps, heading to the parking lot. She didn't see the man directly in front of her until they crashed head-on.

The man took the brunt of the encounter, stumbled back a step and shouted, "Hey, look where you're going, lady!"

Glenda's eyes locked onto the name tag on his uniform shirt: "Lewis."

Glenda said nothing, but in her mind, everything faded away—sounds, sights, smells—it was like there was nothing else in the world except Glenda and the man in front of her. He was looking at her as he regained his balance. What *he* saw was a crazy woman. Her eyes, wide. Her breathing, like a bull ready to charge—short and fast puffs. Her jacket was open, exposing a blood-stained blouse. As he backed away, he forced his eyes away from her face and found the gun. It was in her hand, aimed at his midsection. "What the hell?"

Glenda's voice was guttural. "This pistol is loaded with 410 shotgun shells, and it will blow your guts all over this parking lot," she said. "If you run, I swear to God, I'll pull the trigger and you will die right here on these steps."

"Take it easy," said Tom, trying to remain calm. "I haven't done anything to you. Put the gun down. Please put it down."

As he sputtered, his eyes fell on the phone in her other hand. "Shit! You're her mother."

"Where the hell is she?" hissed Glenda. "You're going to take me to her."

"Look, whatever-your-name-is, she's okay," said Tom. "I swear it. We were going to take her to Nashville—to you actually. She's okay! You don't need that gun."

"Shut up!" yelled Glenda. "We are going to get in my car, and you are going to take me to her. You understand?"

"Sure, lady," said Tom. "But you got this all wrong. We were just trying to help her."

"Move!" snapped Glenda.

She guided him to the car, waving the gun. "Get in," she growled.

Lewis didn't move. Glenda pulled the hammer back.

"Okay, lady," he said as he opened the door and got in on the passenger side. Glenda walked around the front of the car, pointing the pistol at the man through the windshield. Tom Lewis knew she would pull the trigger. She opened the driver's side door, keeping *The Judge*, her pistol, pointed directly into Lewis's face. She closed the door. She had pocketed the phone on her way around, and, once in the car, she brought her left hand up to support the heavy pistol in her right hand—a shooter's position. She asked, "Why did you have her phone?"

"The battery was dead," said Lewis. "I was going to charge it for her, and when she left she forgot it."

"Left for where?"

"Look, she was sick," he said. "A friend of mine said she could stay at his place until she felt better. Then he would drive her home—to you. That's all. So help me God, that's all—you'll see. Look, let me call my friend and tell him we're coming. You can talk to her. See for yourself she's okay."

"First, you give me directions," said Glenda.

"Okay, she's with Rocco Fantini," said Tom. "He has a big house on East Main. The one with a bright blue roof. You can't miss it."

"What kind of place is it?"

"What?"

"You heard me."

"Look lady, I told you. Rocco was going to drive her home."

"What kind of place?"

"You know."

"No, I don't know. What does Rocco do?"

Lewis was sweating. "I told you where she was. Now let me go."

"Just answer my question!" screamed Glenda.

Hesitatingly, Lewis said, "Look, he has girls, but he was going to take your daughter home."

"Get out!"

Lewis wasted no time fleeing the car, slamming the door behind him as he shuffled safely to the other side. Before she punched the gas, Lewis sneered at the woman through the glass, and shouted, "It's a friggin' whorehouse, you bitch!"

Glenda didn't hesitate. She pulled the trigger. The glass in the passenger door exploded. Lewis dropped to his knees.

She spun off, tires screaming as she headed toward East Main and the house with the blue roof.

Chapter 32

She's a Killer!

Sam's call startled Bryan from his go-pill buzz, and it took him longer than usual to respond.

"Bryan, it's Sam."

"I know who it is," said Bryan, "but I don't have anything new to tell you. I've been too busy juggling a thousand things over here."

"I called to tell you to forget about following those breadcrumbs to find missing husband number two. He isn't missing anymore."

"Fantastic," said Bryan. "Where did you pick him up?"

"We didn't exactly pick him up," said Sam. "We found him in Glenda Adams's basement all wrapped up in plastic garbage bags."

"No shit!"

"Right. So, you have one less ball to juggle. After we talked, I sent a team over to the Adams place. It was being worked by the TBI, but we used our Homeland Security card to tag along with their crime scene work. Not only did we find the body, we also found a stash of drugs. Enough to open your own pharmacy. Enough fentanyl patches to last a lifetime. By the way, TBI thinks that's what killed the guy in the garbage bag. It was an easy call since the guy had patches all over his back."

"This kind of puts a new light on things, doesn't it?" said Bryan.

"Damn right, and I have more. Even before we talked last time, I had asked our Boston people to dig up husband number one. They did, and I asked for a rush on toxicology. They tested his hair."

"Let me guess—fentanyl!"

"Yeah, it was off the charts, enough to kill a herd of horses," said Sam.

"So, you're telling me that our little Miss Glenda is a killer?"

"It sure looks that way. Double homicide."

Chapter 33

Type O Blood

Bonnaroo was a blast. Sammie had her first mushroom, and the high was like something out of a movie, a dream. She had never felt anything like it before. Coming down wasn't fun, but Rocco's girls kept her supplied with Percs and weed. Cannabis had never been her thing, but everyone at Bonnaroo was smoking—so she did too. She thought about calling her mother a couple of times, but she was feeling so good, she didn't want the high to end. If she went home, where would she get more pills? That question terrified her—she knew the answer. She liked the way she felt. She liked it all—the pills, the marijuana, and even those delicious mushrooms.

She was so hungry. It must have been the marijuana. The girl with kitchen duty had made pancakes. Sammie was working on her second buttered and syrup-covered stack in the big kitchen. Rocco had joined her at the long harvest table working on his third cup of coffee, asking about the fun time at Bonnaroo. It had been all party time for Sammie. Rocco had made sure of that. She would have to be stupid not to know what Rocco did—what his girls did. But Rocco knew the power of drugs to keep girls like Sammie in just enough denial until it was too late.

They had left Bonnaroo for the house with the blue roof a few times to clean up and get fresh clothes. This time, though, the girls would make sure that Sammie got hooked up with paying customers. When her drug cloud cleared enough for her to realize that she had been a working girl, Rocco would have her. There was never any going back. From then on, it would be drugs and men—men who paid. Rocco knew she was going to make him a lot of money. Tom Lewis had been right.

At the house with the blue roof, Rocco's phone exploded with the sound of an ambulance siren—a special ringtone. He answered the call. Sammie could hear the panic in the other caller's voice but couldn't make out anything they were saying. Rocco shouted, "Doc, slow down! I can't understand you. Who did they dump on you?"

Rocco listened for several minutes and then said, "Well, is he going to make it or not? Come to think of it, why am I supposed to give a shit?"

He was silent for a while as he listened.

"Yeah, I know their blood types—medical, you know. None of them are Type O."

Sammie quickly said, "I'm Type O negative; everybody wants my blood."

Rocco put the phone down and looked at her. "You've given blood before?"

"Yes, all the time. I've given over two gallons of blood. You want to see my card?"

"The doc says he has an emergency," said Rocco. "A patient needs blood or he isn't going to make it. Looks like Bonnaroo will have to wait."

"You mean you want me to donate blood today?" asked Sammie.

"Yeah, you game?"

"I always give through the Red Cross."

"The doctor says he can't wait for the Red Cross," said Rocco. "He needs someone to go directly to his clinic."

In his urgency, the doctor made sure Rocco knew he could pay.

Rocco looked at Sammie and said, "Sit tight for a minute." He walked out of the room beyond Sammie's earshot.

"How much?"

"Listen to me, Rocco," said Dr. Mick. "This guy and his sister are billionaires, and they don't take prisoners. The sister is flying a jet to the Tullahoma airport to pick him up. If I let him die, I'm a dead man. Name your price. I'm desperate."

"The girl is valuable property," said Rocco. "I don't want anything to happen to her."

"Rocco, I need her friggin' blood—her blood is worth a million dollars to me. It's the rest of her body that's valuable to you."

"You haven't seen this one. I could sell her tomorrow for more than a million."

"The doctor thought for only a few seconds. Listen, a million for a little blood, but if anything happens—two and a half million for your loss—cash, no taxes."

"Deal, doc. I need to know if it's okay to drug her up. You know, in case she should decide not to cooperate."

"No. I'm the only one who should give her anything. Whatever you give her would be in her blood. If you must encourage her, you will have to do it the old-fashioned way."

"If you say so," said Rocco.

"We can't keep talking about this, or it will be too late," said Dr. Mick. "I need her here and I need that to happen *now*. I need her on the table with a needle in her arm!"

"Okay, get your stuff ready. We are on our way."

Rocco went back into the kitchen where Sammie was waiting. "Come on. We need to go now."

"You mean to give blood?"

"Yes."

"To the Red Cross?"

Rocco pulled her up by the arm. "We're on our way to the doctor's office. You'll see; it's just like the Red Cross. But, if you are uncomfortable when we get there, I'll take you to the Red Cross facility."

"Who is this for?" asked Sammie.

"It's one of the owners of the clinic the doctor works for—some kind of accident. An emergency. They need us to hurry."

Rocco kept his hand on Sammie's arm, moving her quickly to his car.

The rush was making Sammie nervous. "I need to get home," she said. "Maybe I'll go back to Bonnaroo some other time. You can call the Red Cross. They probably have the blood you need. I'm sure you don't really need me."

"Tell you what," said Rocco calmly. "You give the doc a little of your blood and as soon as that's done, I'll take you back to Nashville. Deal?"

"We go just as soon as I give blood?"

"Right," he said. "Straight away. I promise."

"I guess it's okay. Just a pint, and then we'll leave, okay?"

"Yep, that's my girl."

Sammie was still uncomfortable with the plan, but she had never had a problem giving blood, and now she really wanted to go home. Things just didn't seem right anymore, and her high was wearing thin.

Chapter 34

The Blue Roof

Glenda drove the streets of Manchester looking for her daughter. Suddenly, she spotted the blue roof. The bright metal stood out from its shingled neighbors and made the large old house seem like it wanted to be noticed. An easy landmark if you were giving someone directions: *Just go to the house with the blue roof.* That was all you needed to say if you were telling someone where Rocco's girls were.

She stopped next to the curb and reached for the pistol on the passenger seat of the car. *The Judge* chambered 410 shotgun shells or 45 magnum cartridges. She had used the weapon to shoot the intruder at her home and to rid the world of the lowlife Lewis. She needed to reload. Glenda opened the glove compartment and took out the box of 45 magnums. She ejected the spent 410s and loaded *The Judge* with six personal defense 45 magnum hollow-point cartridges.

With the pistol reloaded, Glenda drove the car up the driveway toward the big house and stopped behind a GMC Yukon with its back door open. It was being loaded with what looked like camping gear. There was no one at the car.

Glenda's eyes filled with tears and her lower lip began trembling. The pain had gotten bad in just the last few minutes. But she couldn't give up now—Sammie was here, and she was going to take her home. She got out of the car and tried to run up the stairs but didn't have the strength. The terrible cramps came in waves and the time between them was getting briefer. The pain in her abdomen was unbearable. She knew the wave of pain would go away in a few minutes but each time it came back it seemed stronger. She didn't have much time left. She was bent over, climbing the steps and fighting the current cramp in her belly. She could feel it slowly unknotting—she needed to hold on until it went away.

Before she could get to the top of the steps, three women with arms loaded for the SUV came out of the door. Glenda was blocking their way. She straightened up as the cramping finally let her out of its grip. "I want my daughter!" she commanded. "Don't lie to me. I know she's here."

A girl with dark brown hair said, "Oh, you must be Sammie's mother. I'm Nancy, by the way."

Glenda didn't return Nancy's smile. She wasn't here to make friends. These people took Sammie. "Where is my daughter?"

Nancy had no idea that the lady she was talking to considered her an abductor. To Nancy, Sammie was just the new person that had joined Rocco's family, as she called it. "She and Rocco went to the clinic to see the doctor," Nancy said.

Glenda was startled. "Why?" she asked quickly. "What's wrong? Is she hurt?"

"No," said Nancy. "I'm sorry, that's not what I meant. She's going to give blood."

"Blood?" cried Glenda. "For God's sakes, why?"

"Some man was hurt and they found out that Sammie has the type of blood they need."

Glenda was surprised at Nancy's matter-of-factness. She didn't act like the bad people Glenda had expected to find at the house. She didn't talk like Sammie was a hostage or prisoner. Yet she knew Sammie would have called her. She *knew* Sammie was being held against her will or she would have called. "Take me there!" she demanded.

"I'll give you the directions," said Nancy. "We were just leaving."

Glenda pulled the gun out of her coat pocket and pointed it directly at Nancy. "First, you will take me to the clinic."

The two women standing next to Glenda's target started to retreat to the door. Glenda shifted her aim and fired. The bullet struck the house just to the right of the doorframe, but the loud report of the 45 had the effect Glenda intended. The women froze in place.

Nancy, screamed, "Shit, you crazy woman! What the hell did we do to you?"

"I told you. I want my daughter."

"Okay!" said Nancy, breathing hard. "The clinic isn't that far. Why do I have to take you?"

"I don't have time for this," said Glenda. "Get in my car—all of you."

Nancy stood her ground. "Look, lady, we are not going anywhere."

The sound of Glenda's two rounds sent Nancy's heart racing. She didn't understand—if she had been shot, there should be pain. She whirled around and realized that the bullets had not been meant for her but for her two friends. Her "sisters." Both were crumpled on the porch and there was blood, a lot of it. She tried to make sense of it. She turned back to Glenda and screamed, "Why, for God's sake—why?"

"Because it doesn't matter anymore," Glenda answered. "Now get in the damn car and take me to my daughter."

There was no more talk. Nancy was shaking, but she did what she was told. She got in Glenda's car. She didn't want to die.

Chapter 35

Mariko

Mariko's search for Sammie had, of course, taken her to the Manchester jail—the last known location of the missing girl. Rollins was sure she was there. Bryan had verified her presence in the visitor room by hacking into security video files and confirming her identity using the facial recognition software.

Mariko knew the jail was the logical place to begin looking for bread crumbs. And crumb number one was the sheriff deputy, Tom Lewis.

When Mariko arrived at the jail she drove into chaos. A large section of the parking lot was a taped-off crime scene. Mariko could see what looked like the entire Manchester force of first responders milling around behind the tape. She saw a lot of long guns and a variety of uniforms orbiting a parked car and a nearby ambulance.

An officer approached Mariko as she sat behind the wheel of her Aston Martin.

"Sorry ma'am, but we've had a shooting," he said

sternly. "We're on lockdown. You're not safe here. Please turn around and leave the area."

"I'm looking for a missing girl," Mariko said quickly. "I think one of your officers knows what happened to her. It's really important. We are concerned for her safety."

"Whatever it is, it's going to have to wait," said the officer. "Now please, do as I said and exit the area."

Mariko spoke again: "One quick question. Do you know where I can find deputy Tom Lewis?"

The officer looked surprised. "What was that name?" he asked.

"Lewis, Tom Lewis."

"What's your business with him?"

"It's about the missing girl," said Mariko. "We think he might know where she is."

Mariko realized that she was tiptoeing around the truth. The circumstances, though, demanded a bolder approach. Her mission was too important not to talk straight.

"Oh, to hell, with it," she muttered under her breath. "We think Lewis is a low-life asshole involved in the girl's disappearance."

The deputy jerked his head back. He was surprised that anyone would speak to an officer about his colleague so bluntly, but he also knew two things. One, Tom Lewis was indeed a low-life asshole, and two, the missing girl might have something to do with Lewis's corpse currently residing in the parking lot.

"I want you to pull over there to your right and park," he said. "Stay in your car. You understand?"

Mariko nodded.

"The sheriff is going to want to talk to you," said the deputy as he turned to walk away.

Mariko called after him. "Tell me what's going on."

The deputy wouldn't normally have offered any information to a civilian, but Mariko seemed to already know some details.

"You see that car over there," he said, pointing.

Mariko nodded.

"Well, that, my little lady, is Tom Lewis's car."

"So, is he here now?" she asked hopefully.

"He *is* here," said the deputy. "Still in his car. But if you were looking to talk to him, lady, you're out of luck. He doesn't have a face left. Someone just blew it away."

"Oh, shit!" said Mariko.

"You can understand why the sheriff is going to want to talk to you, right?" said the deputy, who quickly walked toward the group of officers near Lewis's car.

With her window down, Mariko heard the familiar sound of a large caliber handgun. The shot was far enough away that most people wouldn't have noticed unless they were listening for it or, like Mariko, had been trained to react to the sound of gunfire.

She activated Aurora, the new satellite communication device. She needed to connect to Bryan.

"Tom Lewis is dead," she said as soon as he answered. "Shot in the parking lot of the Manchester jail. To be more precise, a deputy told me his face had been blown away. They want me to wait here, at the crime scene, to be debriefed by the sheriff. But Bryan, I'm sure I heard a pistol shot just now. It was faint, but loud enough to have been somewhere nearby. I think I need to investigate."

Bryan listened in silence, shocked that developments seemed to be getting ahead of him.

"The shit keeps flowing," he said. "Lewis being killed can't be a coincidence. It must be Glenda Adams. I should have gotten this info to you sooner. We now know that she killed both husbands. She also appears to have been the shooter who caused all the carnage at her home. Point is—she is armed and dangerous."

"That certainly puts a new twist on things," said Mariko.

"I don't know what to say," said Bryan. "It is my job keep you current. Not knowing about Adams could have put you in grave danger."

It took a second for Mariko to fully realize that Bryan was right. He had put her in danger by sending her in blind. She had always trusted him to keep her safe. Something was different. She was more confused than angry, but she decided to respond in anger—he had let her down.

"I depend on you to keep me on the right side of the grass," she said. "I should have known about this long before I got to the jail. Nothing bad happened, at least not this time."

She composed herself with a deep breath. Bryan waited silently on the line.

"Here is what you can do for me now," she continued. "Put one of your birds over Manchester. If the Adams woman did this, that means she got here before me, and she and I are both looking for the same thing—her daughter. She's already ahead of me somewhere in this town and she has a handgun with her. We know she has killed with it. I'd like to know there's some backup in the sky if I need it."

"Consider it done," said Bryan.

Mariko continued, "I need to find out where that shot came from."

"The drone should be overhead soon," said Bryan. "It's in the air. I just had to reroute it. If there are more shots, the drone will pick up the muzzle flashes as well as the sound. Good thing you're in a car for a change. I'm directing the drone's video and telemetry to your vehicle's navigation screen—that would have been a little challenging if you had been on one of your flashy bikes."

"It's black as pitch here except for some street lights," said Mariko. "Can the drone see in the dark?"

"It has a night vision camera," said Bryan. "Plus, if you need it, this bird has a very powerful broad beam spotlight. It can light up a football field as bright as a nighttime game. The only problem, though, is the battery drain. I can't keep the light on for long. A minute or two at a time is the best I can do without grounding the bird."

Mariko interrupted, "Something's going on here. I heard two more shots and three of the sheriff's vehicles just flew out of here with lights flashing. I'm going to follow them."

"Hold it," said Bryan. "Stay put for now. They are responding to a 911 call reporting gunshots. Sherlock is monitoring their dispatch radio frequency."

"It's on my car's display now," said Mariko.

"That's from Sherlock," said Bryan. "The drone is still about ten minutes out. I want you to wait until we have the drone over your head."

"My guess is that the gunshots equal Glenda Adams which equals our missing girl," said Mariko. "The sheriff must be headed for the gunshot location—why shouldn't I be on their tail?"

"That's just it," said Bryan. "They aren't going to the right location. They're headed to the place where the gunshot was heard and reported. Let's wait until we get more info. I don't want you in the middle of gun play without having an eye in the sky to give you real-time situational awareness."

"Sorry Bryan," said Mariko. "I can't just stay parked. Your fancy bird is going to have to catch up with me. My current 'situational awareness,' as you called it, tells me that this situation is perishable—meaning if I don't get there before she skips, I'm going to be pissed. The Adams woman is all I've got to lead me to Sammie. Otherwise, I'm in the dark."

"Okay, watch your back," said Bryan.

"I'm depending on *you* for that," said Mariko. "Don't let me down. Keep me on the right side of the grass."

Chapter 36

Bloodletting

Sammie didn't understand. *This isn't the way it's done,* she thought. *Why are they strapping me in?*

She faded out before she could fight or protest. The IV in her arm pulled her into its darkness just as her blood began to flow out from the other arm.

"Hey, doc, what are you giving her?" asked Rocco.

"Propofol."

"Wait a damn minute! Isn't that what killed Michael Jackson?"

"You need to get out of here and let me do my thing, Rocco. I know what I'm doing."

Rocco persisted. "I brought her here so she could give blood, that's all," he said. "I want her back healthy—in one piece, goddammit!"

Rocco realized they weren't alone. He hadn't seen the others when he and Sammie arrived. They must have been in one of the examining rooms. Now a woman stood at the doctor's side along with a nurse who had another two men with her. And, they didn't look like hairdressers. The woman looked at Rocco and said in a slow and calm voice, "That's my brother on the other table. We are taking as much blood as we need. All of it, if that's what it takes."

Rocco immediately protested. "Lady, I don't know who you think you are, but this is my neighborhood. The girl is mine. I'm ending this now."

There was no blood bag. Sammie's blood was flowing directly into the leaking body of the woman's brother. Rocco reached for the IV line in Sammie's arm. The doctor moved to stop him, but it was unnecessary. One of the woman's men got to him first with a crushing blow to the back of his head that sent him sprawling unconscious to the floor.

The man looked at his boss-woman and said, "What do you want me to do with him, Mrs. De La Cruz?"

"Is he dead?"

"Nah. At least not yet."

The doctor said, "You think he's going to forget about this when he wakes up? Like he said, you're in his hood. He'll go screaming to the sheriff. I'm screwed here!"

"Doc, we're all leaving here together," said Lena. "You don't have to come back to this hick town. We'll set you up in Miami. Now shut your face and get my brother ready for a flight out of here."

Rocco moaned. It looked as if he might be regaining consciousness.

Lena said, "Give him a dose of whatever you're giving the girl. I don't want him making more trouble."

"It doesn't work like that," said Dr. Mick. "It has to be continuous; we would have to do an IV."

Lena didn't debate the issue further. She looked at the man on her right and said, "William, take care of the problem."

William obeyed. A quick twist of Rocco's neck broke his spinal cord.

"Good," said Lena. "We'll take him with us in the plane. You can drop him over the water on the way home."

Lena turned to look at the doctor and the very worried nurse. "All right, people, you see how serious this is. We need to get out of here. Do you have my brother ready to fly?"

The doctor was putting a clamp on the IV line, stopping the flow of blood. "I haven't been able to stop the bleeding," he said nervously. "Honestly, I don't know if he is alive. His brain may already be dead. We're just keeping his heart and lungs going."

"That is all I want, Doctor."

"If I take any more blood, it could kill the girl," he said. "But if he keeps on bleeding, without more blood, his body is going to shut down."

"Take all of her blood," Lena said without hesitation.

"I can't do that!" said Dr. Mick. "I'd be killing her."

"I think if you try real hard you can do it," said Lena. "Because if you don't, I will feed you and your pretty nurse to the sharks. *Comprende?*"

A sudden pounding on the door made the room go silent.

Chapter 37

Beating Death

Lena looked at the doctor, "Who the hell is that?"

"No idea." The doctor looked perplexed.

"Get rid of whoever it is," she said.

The pounding grew louder.

The doctor crossed the room to the door. "We're closed," he said abruptly.

Glenda pushed the barrel of her pistol harder against the back of Nancy's head.

"Doc, it's Nancy. I have to see Rocco. Please let me in."

Lena moved to the table where Sammie was strapped down. She removed the clamp that was stopping the flow of blood. She wanted every drop of that blood in Carlos.

"He's not here, Nancy. Please go away."

"His car is here. I know he's in there."

Glenda pushed Nancy aside and fired a round through the door.

Lena's men immediately drew their weapons and went into defensive mode.

Lena moved away from the door.

Doc's hands were on his chest and blood was blooming on his white medical jacket. He staggered back away from the door and fell to the floor.

One of Lena's men fired three rounds at the door, killing Nancy, who Glenda had pulled in front of her as a shield.

Lena shouted, "What do you want?"

"I want my daughter!" screamed Glenda. She fired into the door to drive her demand home.

"This is too much!" shouted Lena, who turned to her men and said, "It's time to go. Kill whoever it is. Kill her now!"

William emptied the rest of his clip into the door—fifteen 9mm rounds, then realized his mistake. He didn't have a second clip.

Jake, the second and older man on Lena's team, with his weapon drawn, moved beside the riddled door. "All right, lady, put down your weapon, or we blow your daughter away."

There was no answer from the other side. William called to this partner, "Hey Jake, you got a spare clip?"

Jake retrieved a backup clip from his shoulder holster and tossed it toward William. "I'm going to open the door. Back me up."

It was a bad toss. William slapped at it, and the clip ricocheted to the right, falling under the medical table holding Sammie. Jake didn't wait for backup. He stood to the side as he partially opened the bullet-ridden door just enough to peer out. He expected to find a dead or wounded woman, and he did—but it was Nancy. Thinking he had killed the girl's mother, he opened the door wider. That was the last thing he ever did. Glenda, who had pressed herself against the side of the clinic wall, fired pointblank into Jake's surprised face. His body fell back into the clinic. His weapon fell to the floor.

Glenda followed his body through the door, killing William as he tried to load the recovered clip into his weapon. Lena stood frozen. Glenda now saw only one thing—her daughter. One thing a cancer patient knows about is IVs. She expertly disconnected the IV that had been dripping the sedative into Sammie's unconscious body and then the tube that had been draining her body. Glenda applied pressure to stop the bleeding that continued from the site of the transfusion needle. As her awareness of the room was returning, she saw Lena picking up the weapon William had dropped. *My gun,* she thought. *Where is my gun?* She had put it down to work on Sammie.

Lena had recovered and was now pointing William's gun at Glenda. She was a businesswoman, after all. She knew when to make a deal.

"Don't so much as move an inch," she said. "You want your daughter. I get that. I want my brother. That's him on the other table. If you want her to live, we will need to work together."

"What have you done to her?" begged Glenda.

"We needed her blood. Doc took too much so you need to get her to the hospital. I can help you, but you must help me too."

"How?"

"Help me get my brother and your daughter in my SUV, and I'll help you get her to a hospital."

Suddenly, they both heard the sirens.

"It sounds like it's too late," said Glenda. "The cavalry seems to be on the way."

"Lady, you seem to forget that you are the shooter. The cavalry is coming to save me—not you."

Glenda said, "It makes no difference; I'm dying, so what can they do to me?"

Lena broke into a loud laugh. When she caught her breath, she said, "Me too! Without his body, I'm dead. I need his heart and his lungs. There's still time if we hurry. Let's get them to my SUV. I have a plane and a doctor waiting. Otherwise, we both lose."

Lena was right, and Glenda knew it. If they didn't work together, she would have already lost. Sammie would die. "Okay, let's do it," she said.

The gun was no longer useful. They either worked together or they both lost. Lena dropped the gun and unlocked the wheels on the table carrying her brother's body. She pushed it out the door and down the ramp. Glenda managed to get her daughter in a wheelchair and followed Lena down the ramp to the waiting Suburban.

They were dealing with deadweight and it took both of them and all their strength to load the unresponsive Carlos into the back of the SUV. Loading the lighter girl was easier. Sammie was still unresponsive. Glenda hoped that it was the lingering effects of the sedative. There was no time to check her pulse.

But the key. The driver was inside the clinic and he was dead. *Where was the damn key?* While Glenda was loading Sammie into the Suburban, Lena went back to sift through the pockets of her dead soldiers. *You lousy asshole,* she thought as she retrieved the key from William's pocket.

Glenda climbed into the passenger seat when she saw Lena running back to the car with the key in hand.

They raced out of the clinic parking lot. Within seconds they saw three sheriff cars approaching with lights flashing and sirens screaming. Lena's street smarts kicked in and she pulled to the side of the road, like a good citizen, to give the cars uncontested right-of-way. They sped by with a fourth unmarked car close behind.

Lena wasted no time after they passed. She was back on the road and accelerating—speeding toward the small airfield with her waiting plane and the on-board doctor who—she hoped—would keep Carlos's heart and lungs alive, even if they had to discard his body.

Chapter 38

More Bodies

Tony put in an urgent call to Mariko. "I still have one good arm," he said. "And I understand you might need some backup, so I'm here in Manchester. Where are you?"

"I'm at the clinic," she replied. "I think you know where that is."

"Right. I'm less than five minutes away. Be there in a sec."

"I'm putting us on conference, Tony."

Bryan responded the minute he saw the message *Aurora incoming* light up on one of the monitor displays in front on him. "Mariko, what's going on? Fill me in."

"Okay, Bryan, but what about Sam? Is he on with us?"

"No," said Bryan. "He's not available right now. Off working on his number one priority."

"Okay, you want to be filled in! Here it is: I'm up to my neck in dead bodies, and I'm at a dead end."

"I get the frustration," said Bryan. "But I need a little more that."

"Right," said Mariko. "I'm with the sheriff's task force who just collected two bodies from the front lawn of what amounted to a bordello in the historic part of the city. None of the working women inside the house knew what went down outside. I called them women but I should have said girls because they were all young—very young. Anyway, I explained about Sammie and Glenda Adams to the sheriff who had taken charge of the crime scene. When the sheriff and I questioned the women inside the house, they acknowledged that Sammie had been there. One of the young girls remembered overhearing their host, some pimp named Rocco, talking about giving blood. That led us to where we are now, the clinic."

"What have you found there?" asked Bryan. "By the way, I have the drone looking down on the clinic now."

"Then you can see two cars in addition to mine and the green and white sheriff's cars," said Mariko. "The mother and probably the daughter were here because one of those cars belongs to Glenda Adams, but there is no sign now of those two people. On the other hand, I have a shitload of recently dead people—the bordello's pimp, that is the other car; plus a woman in a nurse's outfit; what looks like the clinic's doctor; and finally two other men. One of the men is wearing a shoulder holster and the other a fancy Galco Avenger belt holster. They were clearly hired guns. I found three weapons scattered on the floor—two 1911-style automatics, both with 9-millimeter ammo. The third weapon was a big revolver. Its barrel is engraved with the words *The Judge*. It's probably the source of the initial gunshots because the spent shells in it were 45 caliber ammo. I'm assuming it is the weapon belonging to Glenda Adams since the holsters on the dead guys are for the 1911-style automatics."

Bryan made notes as Mariko continued.

"In the final analysis," she said, "aside from the revolver, the car outside is the only solid piece of evidence I have that the woman and her daughter were here. More importantly, I have no clue were to go next. Nothing. The two women must have new transportation so I don't know what vehicle to look for. I'm telling you, this woman may kill everyone in this damn town before I catch up with her or her daughter. We're dealing with a mad woman—as in crazy."

Tony interjected, "Bryan, can't you tell us what vehicle left the clinic shortly before Mariko got there? Surely the drones picked it up."

"They would have if the car left after the drone had reached the area," said Bryan. "I'll review the footage and see what I find. But the vehicle could have departed before the drone reached Manchester. It will take some time."

"We may not have time," said Mariko.

"What about that airplane, Bryan?" asked Tony.

"*What* airplane?" yelled Mariko.

"Tony's right," said Bryan. "I should have been more on top of this. Mariko, you need to head for the private airfield in Tullahoma. I'm sending the GPS coordinates to your navigation screen now."

Mariko's anger was rising. "Obviously, there are some things you've not been telling me," she said. "Bryan, what's up with you? I don't like being kept in the dark!"

"It's not intentional," he said. "Here's the deal: The new software we managed to get on the QT from Sam's people picked up a flight plan filed for a private jet flying from

Miami to a private field in the area. The plane is a Lear registered to the same corporation that owns the clinic you are standing in right now. What caught the attention of the software was that the destination put the plane in the proximity of two possible terrorist targets—Bonnaroo and, more likely, the wind tunnels at Arnold Air Force Base. The air force base is Sam Littleton's number one pick."

"Anything tie this to Adams specifically?" asked Mariko, trying to contain her frustration.

"Well, the flight plan was filed shortly after the CEO, Lena De La Cruz, received a call from your clinic," said Bryan. "The metadata picked up from the call included key words that could suggest a possible connection with the shooting at the Adams residence. I passed the info on to Sam, and he sent some of his people to investigate but they didn't find anything unusual—just a routine visit from a CEO to one of her facilities. The plane's papers were in order and everything seemed fine. So, I dropped it from our list of concerns. Maybe Sam's people were wrong, though. In fact, now it seems very likely they were wrong. Because where is the CEO? Where is Miss De La Cruz?"

Mariko answered the rhetorical question. "Dead or alive she's not here. I can tell you that much. But those two dead guys are, or rather *were*, probably her security detail—bodyguards. My guess is that Miss De La Cruz is providing the new transportation."

Tony butted in. "It has to be a rental. Bryan, you should be able to get the info quickly so we'll know what to look for. Mariko, I'm bypassing you and going straight to the airfield. I'll meet your there."

"Roger that," said Mariko. "I'll bring the cavalry with me—the sheriff and his men."

"I'm sending the drone to Tullahoma," said Bryan. "But I may not be able to position it over the airfield. If I get too close to the air base, they'll shoot it down for sure."

Chapter 39

The Plane

The SUV braked hard at the foot of the stairs leading to the open door of the plane. The horn was blasting in hope of getting the attention of the pilots and the doctor. Lena had tried to call the pilots but got no answer. No one was waiting for them at the stairs and the horn wasn't bringing anyone to the open door of the plane

"Goddamn bastards," she screamed as she opened the door of the SUV. "Where the hell are they? I need help out here!"

Glenda was equally as quick getting out of the car, but Lena was already halfway up the stairs. Glenda suddenly felt someone behind her. It wasn't a good feeling. She started to turn but never finished. The knife sliced silently, severing her spinal cord. Her brain was still alive. She knew for an instant she was dead, held up only by the arms of her assailant. Her final thought was, *I'm so sorry, Sammie*. That was it. There was no more. There hadn't even been time to ask who or why.

In that same moment, Lena was pulled through the door and thrown into the plane's first seat by a man in a ski mask. Another man behind her dropped something over her head and around her throat. She felt it cutting into her. She was held tight against the seat, unable to pull away. She knew that whoever was controlling the thing around her neck could kill her instantly if they chose to. The first man, with both hands on the arms of her seat and his face inches from hers said, "Who are you, bitch?"

Her anger blocked the fear. If she had been free she would have torn his eyes out and stomped him to death with her spike heels. But she was powerless, pushing against the back of the plane's seat to keep the garrote from slicing deeper into her throat. She managed to spit out the words, "What are you doing in my plane?"

"So that's who you are!" The man removed the ski mask as he said, "Well, bitch, it isn't yours anymore. We've taken ownership."

Her interrogator looked up into the eyes of the man at her neck, ready to give him the nod.

Lena yelled, "Wait! You need me!"

"Bullshit. What do I need you for?"

"I have money. Millions in US dollars and drugs—lots of drugs."

"So do we, so do we!" He nodded to the man behind Lena and the garrote sliced through her carotid artery.

Her killers didn't care about the blood. No one was concerned about the resale value of the plane—it was just a weapon, a bullet to be fired at the enemy.

Glenda's killer entered the door. He was clearly the man in charge. He paused briefly, looking at the bleeding corpse. He looked at the man who had given the order that killed Lena and asked, "What about the others?"

"Dead," he said. "They're in the cargo hold along with the explosives."

"Pilots too?"

"Yes, and another crew member or passenger. We think he was a doctor. See all the medical equipment? It looks like they were preparing to receive a patient."

"Yes, two of them. They're in the back of the SUV."

"Alive?"

"I don't think so."

"You want me to check? What about their bodies? Don't we need to get rid of them like the others?"

"No. It doesn't matter anymore. There's no one left to discover them. This is a private airstrip, and they're all dead. Before anyone new arrives to discover them, we'll be in paradise. Close it up. I'll take the controls."

"Our target?"

"It's the same. We strike at the heart of the Great Satan's drone program. Only this time there's no chance of failure."

"Won't they try to shoot us down?"

"No, they will try to save us. I will declare an emergency, then ask to divert to Arnold. At the last minute, we will crash into the building with the wind tunnels and Allah will reward us."

— ʃ —

The single airstrip was both a taxiway and a runway. The plane taxied to the end of the runway and turned around for takeoff. The runway easily accommodated small corporate jets like the Lear, but this Lear wasn't being piloted by an experienced pilot. This time the plane would need every inch of the airstrip, and even then, it would strain to become airborne.

Chapter 40

Fireball

As the Lear labored and finally heaved from the ground, a man who had been patiently waiting now walked from the cover of his hiding place in one of the hangers to the SUV containing the remains of Carlos and the body of Glenda Adams. He had expected to find Lena's body. He now assumed she was aboard the plane, but he was confident that she was no longer among the living.

He smiled and looked skyward at the Lear as it climbed upward. He whispered a message to Lena or her spirit, "I'm sorry, but it wouldn't have worked anyway, my love. I would have seen to that. You would have died on the surgery table. My Arab brothers, Allah bless them, made the transplant charade unnecessary. You would be surprised to know, my dear, that you have made me rich, just as you promised to do. Oh, you don't know, do you? *We are married!*"

The man reached in his jacket pocket and mockingly held up a marriage certificate to the sky.

"Yes, Lena my favorite, according to this document we were married one year ago today," he continued to whisper. "There is no one left to contest our happy event. Happy anniversary, wife, and if you are wondering, I did love you. At least I did at first, but I loved your things more. So, you see, dear, this way I have them all! All the money, all the houses, all the clinics—all of it! It's all mine."

His voice changed aggressively as he spoke to the men on the plane. "That, my idiot Arab brothers, is far more important than your stupid little plan to crash the plane."

He entered a phone number on his iPhone and the Lear erupted in a thundering ball of fire.

The small private airport had closed for the night after the last scheduled arrival. No on-duty personnel were around to see the Lear depart; nor did they see the undocumented flight that brought the hiding man or carried him away after the Lear exploded.

— ƒ —

Mariko and the sheriff's cars pulled onto the airstrip seconds behind Tony. All of them had seen the enormous fireball in the sky followed by the thunder of the explosion milliseconds later. Mariko was sure she had felt the blast even through the protective metal of her car.

They found the SUV and the body of Glenda Adams along with the body of one dead male. A Florida driver's license in the dead man's billfold identified him as Carlos

De La Cruz. They also found Sammie with a pulse—weak, but a pulse nevertheless.

The young girl had no physical wounds except for hematomas on her arms consistent with Mariko's belief that she was the one giving blood at the clinic. The hypothesis was that it was blood for Carlos. Not wanting to wait for an ambulance, the sheriff quickly had the unresponsive girl loaded into one of his cars. It took them less than ten minutes to get her to the emergency room of the nearby Tennova Healthcare facility. New blood was flowing into her veins within fifteen minutes after being found in the SUV by the sheriff's team. Sammie was going to live.

Using their Aurora devices, the case team was in conference mode. Sam Littleton, head of the Nashville FBI office and the chair of the Homeland Security joint task force dealing with terror threats in the region, had just joined the call. Mark Rollins, still in the hospital, was the only member of the case team missing from the conference. Bryan asked the questions.

"What can you tell us?" Bryan asked Sam.

Immediately Sam spoke. "Number one, some of my people are catching hell from me."

"So, you think that plane was under the command of terrorists?" asked Bryan.

"Hell, yes!" said Sam.

"Well, what went wrong? I mean wrong for them."

"Who knows?" continued Sam. "We may find out more when the TBI finishes its investigation. I can tell you that the explosion was too large to have been your typical terrorist aircraft bomb. That entire plane must have been a bomb. It was loaded with explosives. Frankly,

I don't think the TBI is going to find pieces of the plane to examine. It was vaporized."

"You still think the target was Arnold?" asked Bryan.

"No question about it," said Sam. "Moments before the explosion, the Arnold base received a mayday call from the pilot asking to be diverted to their airfields. We think it was just a ruse to put them over Arnold Air Force Base without being shot down by fighters. For security purposes, there's a 24/7 umbrella of fighter jets protecting the base."

"Sam, if the mayday didn't relate to the explosion, what did? What blew up the plane and saved the wind tunnels?"

"It must have been deliberate—or plain stupidity," said Sam. "I'm leaning toward deliberate. Someone detonated the explosives."

"You mean like the heroes of Flight 93 that crashed in Pennsylvania on 9/11?" asked Bryan. "Maybe the De La Cruz woman? A kind of penance for her sins?"

"No, not unless she was part of the plot," said Sam. "We don't think she was. Based on our earlier investigation and background checks of the pilots, we think the plane must have been hijacked—taken over by the terrorists after my people gave the plane a clean bill of health. Probably the De La Cruz woman and her pilots were dead before the plane ever went airborne. The person who blew up that plane triggered the explosives intentionally. It was someone who wanted to terminate the operation and had the trigger device to do it. My money is on someone on the ground."

"Okay, where is that person?" Mariko asked.

Sam pressed on. "As you might have guessed, Mariko, we have a satellite looking down on that area. It is nighttime, so visibility is limited, but we can tell a lot from its night vision capability. Not as much as daytime, but enough to tell you after the airport closed for the night, a small private jet landed. One human image exited the plane and went into one of the hangers. That image, we believe a man, came out of the hanger as the De La Cruz Lear went airborne. After the explosion, the image returned to the second plane and that plane took off. There was no flight plan. We didn't follow the plane by satellite. The plane did not have a responder identifying it, and we didn't get any identifying marks. In short, we have crap when it comes to the answer, *who was he?* But we know Mr. X, as I call him, was there, and I believe he was the person who pushed the button that aborted the terrorist operation. Who knows, he could have been a good guy—even one of us. But if he was, it must be way beyond by my pay grade."

No one said anything for several seconds. Then Bryan spoke up, "Okay, let's put this on pause for now. I say pause because it isn't finished. It won't be finished until we have secured Sammie's safety and well-being. The Chief would want it that way. And second, not until we have identified Mr. X."

Mariko interrupted. "There has to be a number three, Bryan. Those women working in that house—we must do something about them. The man who ran that house, I guess he was their pimp, is dead, so someone needs to step up and help those girls. Hopefully, bring them back into decent society. With their business leader dead, they are going to need a place to live. They need legitimate jobs."

Tony spoke up. "Mariko's right. There's also another thing. The Chief would want us to shut down those pill mill clinics set up in our backyard."

"Okay, I got it," said Bryan. "Mark wouldn't expect us to shut down this case until we have finished the job—all four pieces. Mariko, stay around Manchester to look after Sammie until we can decide what's next for her. You can also get with the sheriff. Work with him to do what you can to resolve the bordello issues. Tony, I want you to come back to base. I need you to get Mark out of the hospital and back on the job. If we are going to find Mr. X and shut down the pill mills, we'll need the Chief back in the command seat."

Chapter 41

Ground Zero

Early on, before Bryan had it fully functional, Sherlock had already proven its worth.

With the help of little orange pills, Bryan continued working around the clock to get the software fully operational. The stimulants were necessary—after all, the military called them "go-pills" to keep soldiers awake when their lives depended on it; not that they kept you operating at your peak. Bryan had not been at his best, and Mariko and the others saw it firsthand. Nevertheless, despite Bryan's lack of sleep, Sherlock was finally fully functional.

The world map on Bryan's workstation display was mirrored to a synchronized wall of flat screen panels on the far wall of the WHC's case room. Using the database from the NSA, Bryan set Sherlock to graphically trace in 3D all related worldwide communications beginning three months before Glenda Adams's first husband's death. The starting point for Sherlock were the key players involved with the New England pain clinic—specifically Glenda Adams and her two husbands, number one and number two. Working from that starting point, Sherlock began graphing lines of communication in 3D on the world map. The program identified contact points communicating with the starting group. It then added those new contact points to the communications being monitored and charted. It would continue to expand the number of contact points plotted and whose communications were being monitored through an arbitrarily set twenty generations of expansion.

As Bryan popped more pills and tried to understand the display, Sherlock continued to build a complex spiderweb of lines representing communication paths between contact points—Bryan's "breadcrumbs." It wasn't long, however, before the spiderweb began to look like a giant pile of spaghetti as Sherlock added layer upon layer of interconnecting lines. The volume of information was overwhelming, and lack of sleep had dulled even Bryan's massive IQ. The picture Sherlock was creating was too big, too deep, too overlapping to make sense out of it. This was more than Bryan could handle. He needed to find a way to simplify the picture. To do that he had to ask the right questions, but that meant he had to know those questions. The go-pills had robbed him of his edge. He knew he needed help—he needed Mark Rollins.

Bryan didn't want to leave the case room and his work with Sherlock, so he sent Tony and Big John to the hospital in one of the WHC SUVs. He gave them an order: "Bring Mark back to the club. Bring him back even if you have to fight the hospital staff or carry him to the SUV."

When they returned, Big John pushed Mark's wheelchair into the case room and parked him next to Bryan who was still pressing Sherlock to give him the answers he was looking for. Tony got Mark a glass of water.

Mark sat quietly staring at the displays on the conference room wall while Bryan explained the software and its capabilities. "Also, Chief, keep in mind that what we are watching has already taken place," he said. "We are replaying communication activity and, of course, it is sped up. Sherlock displays a day's worth of activity in just a few seconds."

"Thanks for that briefing," said Mark. "It helps, but I see the problem. Sherlock is almost too good. It's feeding us more information than we can digest. We need to get rid of background noise."

"What do you mean?" asked Bryan.

"We don't need more information. We need less," said Mark. "We only need contact points and communication that is clearly relevant to our interests. Everything else is just background noise and we need to get rid of it. Can you tell Sherlock to ignore everything except what is specifically related to our issues? By that, I mean *illegal drugs, controlled substances, human trafficking, prostitution, and security threats including both terror and criminal activity*. We only want to see contact points where at least one of the involved parties has a history involving our areas of concern or where the content of the communications has keywords related to those issues."

Bryan's hands were already keying instructions into Sherlock as he answered Mark, "Yeah, Chief, I can do that."

Sherlock then began to isolate the activity relevant to areas of concern identified by Rollins, eliminating unrelated activity, "background noise." The display at the front of the conference room cleared. After just a few seconds, the world map reappeared and Sherlock began adding contact points and lines of communication starting from a single bright spot in the New England area. Then a line shot out to southern Florida and, like a flash of lightning, a spiderweb of lines began to grow from a center of activity in southern Florida location—a location in Miami.

As tangled as the lines were, each told a story. The images on the map were like those an aircraft controller sees on his or her screen. Each line had embedded tags telling the direction of the communication and the means of delivery.

"I can click on the line for drilled-down access to the content of the communication starting with keywords," Bryan explained. "And, if needed, I can retrieve the full content of the communication between both parties. Contact points, or what I call breadcrumbs, are identified by a Sherlock-assigned alphanumeric code. If I click on, or enter, the code number, Sherlock will display information about the contact point as well as its GPS coordinates. Another click and I can access the latest satellite still image or, if available, a real-time satellite view of the location. If the contact point can be attributed to individuals, Sherlock identifies those individuals; and with a few more clicks, it will deliver a detailed dossier."

As the men watched, Sherlock continued the spinning of a delicate web, the lines crisscrossing the United States. As the communication date moved closer to the present time, a line shot from Miami across the image of the globe to somewhere in the Middle East. From that single contact point, there was a burst of zigzagging communication lines to and between contact points elsewhere in the Middle East and Europe. A completely new group of relationships was evidenced by the distinct web of relevant activity between contacts outside of the United States, but with a Miami central connection.

Mark suddenly rose in his seat. "Bryan," he said, "pause Sherlock for a minute!"

"Okay, done, Chief."

"I don't like what we're seeing on the screen," said Mark. "Miami seems to be the center of things. Let's see what we are dealing with. Bring up that location on your display."

Bryan clicked on the location ID. Sherlock displayed a satellite view of the location most relevant as the center of communication activity. It was a sprawling estate set back far behind what appeared to be a high stone wall covered on the street side by dense vegetation. A heliport was centered in the green lawn, an otherwise open field between the mansion and its street-side protective barrier.

Bryan couldn't help noting the defensive layout. "Chief, anyone in that open field would be an easy target. A couple of shooters in the mansion could hold off an army trying to cross that field. It would be a shooting gallery even for a tiny defending force."

"I suspect that was the idea," said Mark. "The place is clearly not your average weekend Florida getaway. Let's see what's happening in the mansion's backyard."

"Roger that."

Using his mouse like a joystick, Bryan moved the satellite image toward the area to the rear of the building. The house sat on the edge of Biscayne Bay. Two high-speed cigarette boats stood at the ready, moored at the small dock only steps from the home's back veranda. Watson Island out in the bay was close enough from the shore for the occupants to see the Miami Seaplane Base.

"Chief, this setup looks like plan B to me," said Bryan. "Plan A is that helicopter in the front. It looks like they are prepared to flee that place in a hurry—24/7. If they can't get to the helicopter because they are under assault from that direction, they switch to plan B and exit by speedboat out to sea or just over the bay to the island and one of those seaplanes."

"I think you've nailed it," said Mark. "It's a perfect setup for people engaged in criminal activity. But what about terrorism? If this is the center of a very profitable business involving legal drugs, even if they are prescribed for illegal purposes—why get involved with terrorist activity? We need more answers."

Bryan closed the satellite connection and returned to Sherlock's chart of contact points and lines of communication.

Bryan could feel his energy level and concentration dropping as his session with Rollins continued. As soon as possible, he needed another go-pill.

Chapter 42

Case Closed

Mark Rollins had pressing questions.

"Bryan, there's one thing I don't understand," he said. "I assume a lot of communication was by cell phone. How are those cells tied to a specific location?"

"Sherlock has multiple modes for tracking cell phone communications," said Bryan. "The fastest method is what we're using now. It's not the most accurate, but for getting the big picture, it's good enough. In this mode, the address given at the time of the phone purchase in a normal transaction is used, unless the initial pattern of use is significantly different, in which case it is treated the same as a burner. In the case of burners, the most likely location is estimated based on the pattern of initial use. There are two other modes. We can follow cell phones as they move from cell to cell; or for even higher accuracy, we can pinpoint the actual location of a cell phone at the time of each contact by vectoring off multiple cell towers."

"Okay, I've got it," said Mark. "Humor me for a minute, Bryan. Select one of those Middle East contact points, and let's follow it from cell to cell."

"Sure thing, Chief. Let's use the initial contact—the breadcrumb. The one dropped in the capital of Iran—Tehran. We will start with the first outgoing Miami contact."

The screen cleared and a few minutes later, Sherlock displayed the initial communication from Miami. The cell location remained the same or in nearby cells for some time while the Tehran breadcrumb continued to communicate with other locations in the Middle East and Europe. A few days before the plane explosion incident in the United States, there was a second incoming communication from Miami. That call was quickly followed by an outgoing commutation to four locations within the Middle East. The four contact points were among Tehran's prior communication partners. Within hours the Tehran breadcrumb started to move. The rapid movement from cell to cell indicated that the contact was traveling either by car, bus, or train. Then it became stationary for some time and abruptly went dead.

"What just happened?" asked Mark.

"The towers are no longer picking up signals from the phone," said Bryan. "Our breadcrumb seems either to have destroyed the phone, pulled its battery, or put it in one of those signal-blocking Faraday bags. The bags block out all electromagnetic energy. Michael Faraday invented what he called his Faraday cage in 1836. Now they are cell phone accessories for people like our guy who don't want to risk having their cell phones tracked."

"He's being cute!" said Mark. "Let's see if we can outsmart him. Change to the vectoring mode. I want to know exactly where he was when the phone went dead."

"Right, Chief."

In a few minutes, Sherlock displayed the answer. The cell was in the Mehrabad Airport about thirty-seven miles outside of Tehran.

"Well, Chief, there's your answer," said Bryan. "It looks like he was waiting to board a plane, but I'm afraid we've lost him."

"Not so fast, Bryan. I have an idea, if your cunning software is up to the task. Can you look for a new phone that comes online for the first time—one in the same location as our dead phone?"

"We can scan phone traffic coming out of the airport," said Bryan. "And Sherlock will tag any previously unregistered phone, a burner."

"Okay, give it a try."

Bryan started typing. He had been operating at high speed all morning, but now he could feel his energy fading. The screen cleared. Then new dots began to appear, each representing a phone, one of which was flashing. Bryan clicked on the flashing ID. Sherlock info disclosed that phone had no previously known location—a burner, coming online for the first time.

"Well, Chief, you guessed right," said Bryan. "Look at that timestamp. The new burner came online in the same area just minutes before the phone we were tracking went dead. It appears that our breadcrumb got himself a new phone."

"Great!" said Mark. "Let's switch back to the cell-to-cell mode and see where that new phone is leading us."

The new phone remained in the same location for several hours and then began moving again. This time the cell-to-cell move was extremely fast for a brief period and then disappeared.

"Chief, I think that he's aboard his flight and his signal was lost once the plane reached altitude."

"Right," said Mark. "Check the airport. What flight just left and where is it heading? I'm betting a thousand I can tell you what you're going to find."

Even if Rollins's betting offer had been real, Bryan wouldn't have taken it. He needed another go-pill. "I need to take a short break," he said. "Nature is calling."

"I can use a break too," said Mark. "If you see Tony or Big John, have them check with me."

Bryan took advantage of the break to take another pill. The time between pops was getting shorter. The shot of adrenaline they provided was having a smaller and smaller impact on his system, but he still desired the upside rush after downing one. And he increasingly dreaded the crash. He knew he was getting close to his limit. He needed sleep soon. When he returned, Rollins was back at the conference table with coffee and a sandwich.

"Bryan, Tony brought us food and coffee, if you're interested. They're on the buffet behind you."

"Thanks," said Bryan. "Maybe I'll get some in a minute."

Bryan quickly keyed more commands into Sherlock. After several minutes he stopped abruptly and said, "I got something, Chief. It looks like there was an Air France flight to Paris at that time." He started rapidly keying again. "Give me a few more minutes."

As Bryan continued hammering on his keyboard, Tony came in the room, poured a cup of coffee, and put it beside Bryan's workstation. Bryan paused long enough to take a sip and then said, "I'm in the Air France system—there is one passenger ticketed to Miami via a connection in Paris. That's the name up on the screen. My guess, however, is that the name isn't useful to us. He's probably flying on a phony passport with a phony name. I'll try doing some research to see if we can accurately ID him; but for now, we can at least track him when he lands, as long as he holds on to his new phone."

Rollins took a long look at his number one brain trust.

"Bryan, where's your head, man?" he said. "Have you forgotten? The man is already dead. I don't know what you've been taking, but whatever it is, you need to stop, *now*!"

Mark reminded Bryan that the man—the one he was talking about following when he landed in Florida, was *dead*. Died in the explosion of the plane that he and his pals hijacked.

"We are looking back in time at things that have already taken place," said Mark. "If we followed the track taken by the other four contacts, we would find that they also got on a plane headed for Miami. And from there, they were shuttled to Tullahoma where they killed Miss De La Cruz and took over her plane. All those men, the terrorists, are dead!"

"Oh, my God! You're right," he said. "How could I have let this happen? I got caught up. It was like what we were watching was really happening right now. I wasn't thinking clearly. It had to have been the go-pills—you know what they give pilots. If they give them to pilots, I didn't think they would be a problem. Could they?"

"They are drugs, Bryan. Dope, on the street, they would be called speed. They could be pure amphetamine or any number of other stimulants. Probably a mixture. But you have no business being on those things. For your sake and the sake of those people on our team who depend on you, this needs to stop, and it needs to stop now!"

"Right, Chief. The pills were a crutch. I thought I could handle them. I can't. I see that now. You don't have to worry. There will be no more go-pills, I promise."

"Okay, we all make mistakes, Bryan. Drugs like opioids and that stuff you were taking will destroy that brain of yours. I'll take your word on this—no more experimenting with mind-altering drugs. Agreed?"

Bryan said, "I've learned my lesson. I agree—no more pills unless it's an aspirin. But what do we do about this thing?" Bryan asked, waving at the display screens still showing output from Sherlock.

"I think I've seen all I need to see, Bryan. That exploded plane wasn't a random hijacking. It was orchestrated by someone connected to that location in Miami. And that someone, Mr. X, I think for reasons of his own, pushed the button that blew that plane out of the sky. This is a lot bigger than a missing girl and a pill mill. Everything that we've been dealing with, the New England murder of husband number one, the missing girl, Glenda's rampage, the pill mills, the explosion of the airplane—all of it—has brought us to this point, to that Miami location. A location in communication with contact points in a part of the world that is at war with the United States. Miami is the answer to all of it. It is ground zero for everything we've been dealing with. And Miami is where Mr. X will be found. When that happens, we can finally put all this behind us—case closed."

Chapter 43

Sperry's

We found the girl. Glenda Adams was gone. Everything else had spiraled way beyond the standard WHC brain trust cases. So, we turned our findings over to the FBI to wrap things up.

Tony fully recovered from his injuries and was back in the driver's seat of Black Beauty. Actually, Black Beauty III. This time it's a modified Lexus LS 460 F Sport, complete with armored sides and bulletproof windows. Like its predecessor, Black Beauty II, it has a few built-in offensive systems, some perhaps not-so-legal. Bryan Gray supervised the modifications and turned the car into a high-tech mobile office. Again, I didn't ask too many questions.

Tony, Mariko, Bryan, Sam Littleton, Meg, and I were at Sperry's for a private lunch—our tradition after one of our adventures has ended. While we regularly solve problems for WHC members, most are insignificant as things go. They certainly don't always involve life-and-death issues as was the case in the Glenda Adams adventure. Glenda, it turned out, wasn't exactly the girl I remembered. Mental illness going back to her postpartum experience coupled with a long-term addiction to OxyContin had done away with that girl. Once they threw the terminal diagnosis at her, all the normal rules we live by fell away. Killing a husband she had begun to hate seemed to her the right thing to do. As for husband number two, he was stealing from her accounts. That sealed his doom. As for the rest, as she said, it just didn't matter anymore.

They know me at Sperry's, so a perfect Belvedere martini—dry, straight up, and with olives on the side—arrived at the table as I sat down. Several months had passed since we last got together as a team. Once dessert had been cleared away, I took the opportunity to bring everyone up to speed with what transpired during those months.

"Mariko, you've been the point person taking care of our new ward, Samantha Miller. Of course, to us she is Sammie. Mariko, the table is yours."

"Thanks, boss. As everyone knows, Sammie recovered from the transfusion incident. You may not know that she will wind up penniless despite her mother's substantial wealth. The courts placed everything in escrow while it hears several wrongful death cases. No one really expects anything to be left. The Chief got himself named as her guardian, although that's a duty we all agreed to share. She detoxed while recovering in the hospital and is currently undergoing drug rehab at the Betty Ford Clinic in Rancho Mirage. She's planning to enroll in Middle Tennessee State University after she finishes her stay at the clinic. Right now, she's planning on a double major—computer science and drone management. Bryan spent a lot of time with her while she was in the hospital. He promised her a job on his team if she maintains a 3.5 GPA. Once she detoxed, I discovered just how smart she is. I wouldn't be surprised if she finished at the top of her class."

"After my experience with go-pills," Bryan added, "I understand how easy it is to fall prey to drugs. I didn't have to sleep or eat when I was on them. I knew to take another pill when my feet started to feel the floor again. When I was on those little pills, I just felt like I was floating—light on my feet. When I look back now, I remember the mistakes I made that put Mariko and Tony in danger. It also took me twice, maybe three or four times longer than it should have to get that software fully operational. The worst part is that I, Bryan Gray, didn't want to stop taking them. They made me feel like superman. However, I wasn't anywhere close to the top of my game. Sammie is a strong girl to get off the stuff the way she has. She's smart to go to the Betty Ford Clinic so that she will never go back on the stuff."

"What about those awful clinics?" Meg asked. "The drugs they were writing prescriptions for might be legal, but not for the reasons they were giving them to their would-be patients. Those doctors are no better than the drug dealers pushing amphetamines or heroin on the streets."

"Meg's right," said Tony. "And what about the mystery man we think caused that plane to explode—Mr. X?"

"The clinics are gone," I said. "Shut down. For that and the Mr. X story, I'll turn the table over to Sam."

"Thanks, Mark. As for Mr. X and the drug diversion criminal enterprise, the FBI acted on information supplied by you guys and began an investigation into the now-deceased De La Cruz family. The investigation led to one Fares Bishara who identified himself as the widowed husband of Lena De La Cruz. Bishara and his associates were thought to be the current occupants of the De La Cruz mansion and Bishara, as Lena's alleged heir, was considered sole owner of the Good Comfort Pain Management Clinics.

"The FBI's investigation, however, disclosed that the marriage never took place and the related documents, including the marriage certificate, had been forged. Bishara had not yet applied for citizenship based on his falsified marriage. His visa had long ago expired. Mr. Bishara, a Syrian national, was thus an illegal alien. Based on the FBI's investigation of the Good Comfort Pain Management Clinics, the De La Cruz family, and Mr. Bishara, the Justice Department determined that they constituted a criminal enterprise engaged in the diversion of legal drugs.

"The FBI issued arrest warrants and search warrants and, in cooperation with local authorities, raided the De La Cruz mansion. The action was carried out in a military-style night raid. Authorities first eliminated all opportunities of escape—securing the helicopter in the front of the mansion and the boats in the rear. The surprise raid met with no resistance and for good reason. All they found were bodies—Mr. Bishara, aka Mr. X, and five individuals previously identified by the FBI as among his associates. Still missing are two other Bishara associates expected to have been in residence at the mansion. To date, their whereabouts are still unknown."

Tony gasped. "My God, Sam, who got to them? And how do you know he was Mr. X?"

"As for who got to them, we don't know for sure and probably never will," said Sam. "But the CIA is represented on our joint task force. All that would have been necessary is for a friendly asset in Syria to suggest that the Arnold operation was sabotaged by Bishara. Especially if that word were given to some relatives of one of the martyrs who died on the exploded plane. The murders—or executions—appear to have been an inside job. Perhaps our two missing Bishara associates, for example. It's likely they were plants. In my opinion, whoever killed Bishara and his men did the taxpayers a favor. Putting guys like them on trial is expensive and time consuming—and it opens up the country for more attacks by radicals. We don't need any of that. I only hope the executioners fled the United States after taking their revenge, never to return."

"But what about the clinics?" repeated Meg.

"The federal government confiscated all real property and other assets of the deceased De La Cruz family, including their companies and business enterprises," continued Sam. "All the clinics have been closed. The medical equipment was donated to legal aid organizations and the buildings and land are being auctioned. Drug diversion charges have been brought against all involved doctors for illegally writing prescriptions for controlled substances. Prosecutors anticipate all will be found guilty—lose their medical licenses and serve long prison sentences. In addition, charges are pending against several pharmacies working as accessories to the diversion activities. Some for knowingly looking the other way, and others for active involvement."

After Sam finished his briefing, I knew the team wanted to hear more. You do a lot of second-guessing after an experience like ours. Our tradition of getting together at Sperry's acts as a sort of closure, a crucial step in putting the past behind us. But none of us could move past this as long as there was still a question about Mr. X. As the team's leader, I couldn't let Sam off the hook.

"Sam, what about the rest of Tony's question?" I asked. "Are you sure Bishara was Mr. X and, if so, why did he blow up the plane?"

"We're sure," Sam replied. "Bishara was a plant himself. The Islamic radicals wanted in the drug business. Bishara was implanted in the De La Cruz circle of friends. The original plan may have been to learn the trade, or it might have been to take over the business from the start. We don't know which for sure. As for the wind tunnel plot, we know he received marching orders from somewhere in Germany—orders to help the martyrs in their mission to attack."

Bryan interrupted. "Sam, why didn't Sherlock flag the call from Germany?"

"Actually, our Locard version of the software did," said Sam. "But only because we were looking for it well after the explosion. You missed it because it didn't fall within the parameters you gave the software. The message was deeply coded. The location and the caller were pristine—no prior history connecting them to radical Islam."

"I got it," said Bryan. "Sorry for the interruption. Give us the rest of the story, Sam."

"Based on what we've been able to uncover, it looked like the De La Cruz woman and Bishara initially had a thing going," said Sam. "They were a pair for a while. But somewhere along the way, Bishara appears to have settled on a plan to take over the drug business and was looking for a way to safely do away with the De La Cruz twins. Assisting the terrorists with their plot was never related to the drug takeover plan. But the two missions merged on the night of the plane explosion. Bishara probably thought Allah worked in mysterious ways when Lena got the call from the Manchester clinic. He hurriedly arranged for an off-the-books flight to transport the terrorists to that Tullahoma private airport where the terrorists killed Lena and took over the plane as their weapon to destroy our wind tunnels."

Tony interrupted again. "But why blow the plane?"

"Do you remember the movie *The Treasure of the Sierra Madre?*" asked Sam.

"Sure, with Bogart and John Huston's famous little dance. Who doesn't?"

"Well, there's your answer," Sam continued. "Bishara had gold fever. With Lena dead, he became a multimillionaire. There was no one to contest the marriage or the will he had forged. The De La Cruz horde of cash, all their property, including the business, was his. The hijacking of her plane was the perfect cover protecting him from being accused of Lena's murder. However, the terrorist plans threatened all that. If they succeeded, Bishara knew the government would leave no stone unturned in their investigation. He was afraid the plot would be traced back to him. The certainty of real-world gold had far more appeal than the uncertainty of seventy-two virgins waiting for him in the afterlife. So, he pushed the button!"

Meg's phone suddenly sounded an incoming call. She answered and, after a brief pause, said, "Dad, it's for you. It's a call to the WHC's after-hours emergency number. It's my turn to have the calls forwarded to my cell. The caller asked for you."

Meg handed me the phone.

"Hello, this is Mark Rollins."

I heard a panicked voice on the other end. "Mr. Rollins, I'm in trouble. I need help. There is no one else who can get me out of this spot. I need you, Mr. Rollins. I need your help!"

— ∫ —

The adventures continue.

Selections from Previous Mark Rollins Adventures

Mark Rollins' New Career and the Women's Health Club
Copyright © 2008 M. Thomas Collins

Chapter 4

Tuesday Morning

It turned cold during the night; at least it was cold for Nashville. The thermometer read 28 degrees outside and a comfortable 71 degrees inside. I was having my every-other-morning breakfast: Cheerios topped with banana slices and a dozen or so raisins with 1% milk plus my usual one cup of coffee per day. Not that the Starbuck's crowd would consider the stuff I drink coffee. Believe it or not, I prefer instant to the real thing.

The breakfast room TV, an LCD, was on Channel 5. I wanted the weather forecast. You have to first pay the price of listening to the anchor recount the overnight home invasions, shootings and convenience store robberies. The bad stuff happens in what the newspeople euphemistically refer to as "South Nashville." Tragically, the description of the victim and the perpetrator usually begins with the words "a black man" or "a Hispanic man." There was something different this morning. I heard the anchor say "Belle Meade." I heard it too late to get the details of her report. Someone was missing and there was something said about the Women's Health Club. Whatever the story, I needed to know the details. I left the

Cheerios to get soggy and moved to my home office. My Dell notebook is always on and connected to the Internet for e-mail so it took only a second to find the story on Channel 5's website:

> A wealthy Belle Meade businessman is reported missing. Michael Webb, the CEO of New Visions Investments, a Nashville-based private investment bank, disappeared from his Belle Meade home sometime Saturday morning according to his wife, Elizabeth Webb. Mrs. Webb left her home for an appointment with a personal trainer at the Women's Health Club in Brentwood. Michael Webb who collects classic cars was working on a restored Mustang at the time. Mrs. Webb reported that upon her return home around 3:30 p.m., she found a note from her husband. The note indicated that he had some errands to take care of and then a business meeting that would include dinner. He instructed his wife not to wait up for him. When Mrs. Webb awoke Sunday morning to find that her husband was not in the house, she went to the couple's large carriage house that served as a garage and storage area for Mr. Webb's classic car collection.
>
> Mr. Webb's Jaguar, the automobile he customarily drives, was parked in its usual place. The Mustang, however, was missing. According to Mrs. Webb, her husband's tools

were uncharacteristically scattered around the area. She also observed wipe cloths that appeared to be bloody and what she thought were blood splatters on the floor of the facility. At that point, she called the police.

During a news conference, Chief Carl Morgan indicated that, at the present time, the police have no explanation for the disappearance. Chief Morgan said, "Anyone knowing the whereabouts of Michael Webb or has seen the missing car should contact the Nashville Police Department. The car is very distinctive. It is a powder blue 1965 Ford Mustang convertible in showroom condition with Tennessee license plate number WEB-07."

In response to questions, Morgan indicated that attempts to reach Michael Webb via his cell phone had been unsuccessful.

The Channel 5 story gave me a bad feeling. There are two missing men a husband and a personal trainer—our personal trainer. Elizabeth Webb left her husband at home for an appointment with her personal trainer at our club. Was Rob her trainer? Is there a connection between Rob's disappearance and the disappearance of Webb? The thought was disturbing.

I gave Sarah a kiss and headed for Black Beauty and a quick trip to the WH Club. Black Beauty is my slick Lexus LS sedan with all the bells and whistles and a few non-standard ones added by my IT brain trust. Some of the stuff would make 007 proud.

Fifteen minutes later I pulled into the back lot of the WH Club. It was 6:15 in the morning but there were already 15 or 20 Jags, BMWs, and Mercedes in the lot. I spotted Meg's copper colored Mini Cooper in its usual spot. Meg is who I wanted to see this morning—and the sooner the better.

Mark Rollins and the Rainmaker
Copyright © 2009 M. Thomas Collins

Chapter 6

Ramiro Melendez

Ramiro Melendez was in the US illegally, but he was hardly welcome in his own country. He was on the run from Mexican authorities after jumping bail. His rap sheet starts at age nine when the local grocer had him arrested for shoplifting. But it was his latest predicament that sent him to the US. He killed a man. As Ramiro saw it, the guy had it coming to him, and it had been a fair fight—but he had been the brother of a member of the State Chamber of Deputies.

Ramiro's attorney was an American lawyer. Ramiro wasn't stupid; he reasoned that an American lawyer living in Mexico and working in a "nothing" Mexican law firm meant that his lawyer probably couldn't live or practice law in the US. He was right. After his lawyer managed to get him out of jail on bail by bribing a local judge, Ramiro and his lawyer worked out a deal.

The Melendez family was not poor. Ramiro didn't steal out of need. Stealing was easier than working. Lying was easier than honesty. When Ramiro wanted something, he wanted it immediately. The idea of working hard and saving for things never entered his mind. Ramiro was a long-time problem for the Melendez family so when he asked for money to leave the country, they were only too happy to contribute. Most of the hundred thousand pesos went to Ramiro's lawyer. The lawyer supplied him with documents—a US birth certificate, Social Security number, and a Tennessee driver's license. Except for the birth certificate, the documents were not forged; they were authentic. Ramiro's lawyer had connections in Tennessee. Even in the US, you can find underpaid government employees willing to do things for a little extra money. Tennessee drivers' licenses—genuine licenses—are for sale if you know the right employee. Ramiro didn't know which one, but his lawyer told him that someone who worked in a Memphis Driver's License branch would issue a license to anyone for $500. You send them $500, a name, address, and photograph, and they will deliver the license with no questions asked. There was one other part of the deal. Ramiro was to check in with his lawyer monthly. Why? As the lawyer explained, there might come a time when Ramiro could do the lawyer a favor—one that would put money in both their pockets. Ramiro Melendez found his way to Tennessee and eventually blended into the predominantly Hispanic Nashville community, Antioch. He worked part-time on different landscaping crews but only long enough to identify targets for his more lucrative craft. He was a good thief and his hunting grounds were always in upscale neighborhoods. He picked easy targets. Power tools, chainsaws, and bicycles from unsecure garages provided spending money. The real money was in jewelry and watches stolen from unlocked homes while the husband was away at work and the wife was working in their flowerbeds or gardens.

Ramiro wasn't stupid; but his victims were. He got a good laugh when he thought about it. Their homes always had signs posted warning about their security systems, but the alarms were never turned on during the day. That is when he did his work. He stayed away from night work or homes where the people appeared to be away on trips or vacation. That is when alarms were set. He picked houses where the lady was working in her garden. Those were easy and quick. He would slip into the house and find the master bedroom. There was always a jewelry box. He would grab the most expensive looking things and get the hell out *pronto*! He never spent more than five or ten minutes doing a job. He was long gone before the robbery was ever discovered. He liked it even better when there were landscaping people working on the grounds. He could walk right into the house without anyone noticing. If there should be someone inside the house, he would go into his "*agua* routine." He would become a poor hard-working Mexican looking for water—who apologetically doesn't speak the language. They would quickly send him out of the house, but no one ever called the cops. It always worked. They were stupid; he wasn't.

Ramiro watched the local news because he wanted to see if the newspeople ever talked about his robberies. They never did. But he *did learn* why his lawyer was in Mexico. The woman the lawyer had been living with had disappeared. People think she is dead—and they think the lawyer did it—but they haven't found her body. The unsolved case continues to be talked about on the evening news. The police want to question the lawyer but can't get to him in Mexico. The missing woman's parents are keeping the case alive. They say they want justice. Ramiro thinks they want revenge, and he thinks there might be some money opportunities for him. He decides to find out where the woman's parents live. He may want to have a discussion with them at some point.

Mark Rollins and the Puppeteer
Copyright © 2009 M. Thomas Collins

Chapter 6

"Ding Dong"

"Mr. Nelson, I just learned about Lansden!" shouted Gordon Seemann.

"Yeah, the "great litigator" is dead. Makes you want to sing, doesn't it?" The man laughed and began chanting, "Ding Dong! The old barrister is dead. Which old barrister? The Wicked Barrister! Ding Dong! The Wicked Barrister is dead." At the end of his out-of-tune ditty, he asked, "Has a nice ring to it, doesn't it?"

"Mr. Nelson, the man is dead! Aren't we being a little too flippant about it?" Seemann wondered if Nelson had gone over the edge.

Keith Nelson was fifty-eight. He was a big man, seated behind a big desk in a big office. He had worked on Wall Street most of his life. Million-dollar bonuses had been amassed into an even bigger fortune. He needed that fortune to support his lifestyle. Now, with a new wife and just when he was beginning to enjoy that wealth, it was all at risk—at risk because of that stubborn-ass country lawyer, Lansden, out to make a name for himself.

When the housing boom really started taking off, Nelson was smart enough to see the mortgage refinancing opportunity. With interest rates on the decline and home values skyrocketing, the new generation of homeowners had discovered they could turn their homes into an ATM machine. They could get ready cash to pay down credit cards or other bills just by refinancing. So what if that meant higher mortgage payments? They could just run up the credit cards again and in a couple of years do another refi. Nelson saw that he could pocket big fees by handling the paperwork and passing the risk on to others.

He left the investment firm and started his own mortgage company, Hudson Bluff Mortgage, Inc. The system was rigged, and he saw that it was a game you could not lose. He used to say, "I don't take the risk, just the profits." Get him talking, and he would let you know how it is done. "You close a refi deal. You sell that paper to some dumb-as-hell bureaucrat. You take that money and make more deals. You just do it over and over again. That is all we do—turn the money and take the profits. The bureaucrats bundle the mortgages into $100 million packages that the people on Wall Street are all too happy to sell—for a fee—to institutional and fund investors all over the world. Then the money flows back into the mortgage refi market. It is just one big recycling of money. Everyone is happy. Everyone is making money." . . . "That was until the shit hit the fan," he later said.

"Gordon, you don't understand! You should be celebrating. Your butt has just been pulled out of the fire. That bastard, Lansden, had us by the balls over the Fenio mortgage case. Hell, Fenio hocked his house to start a bunch of taco stands—refinanced their place for a hell of a lot more than it was worth. He didn't even have a job. Lost his shirt—and, when the bank was foreclosing,

Fenio's wife goes running to the Great Harold T. Lansden claiming we shouldn't have loaned the damn money! We are supposed to have told Fenio it was okay to lie like shit on the application. Lansden was going to sue us for the big bucks!

To hell with the money—after he got through with the two of us, I figured we would be damn lucky to stay out of jail. Hell, we were both going to be ruined by that hillbilly. I'm the CEO; you're the CFO. We are the people the public wants to see swinging from a lamppost. We are the "corporate fat cats." Obama, that damn Congress, and the fucking news media has whipped our dumb-as-a-post citizens into a pitchfork marching mob. This time they aren't after Frankenstein—they want a piece of you and me. They want to stick those pitchforks into some mean, bad corporate executives!"

Gordon Seemann was a young CPA. He joined the staff of a large national CPA firm right out of college. Three years later, he was the senior member of the audit team assigned to the Hudson Bluff Mortgage, Inc. account. It was Seemann's job to review the accounting firm's proposed management letter with Mr. Nelson before issuing the final report to the Board of Directors. The initial draft had been strongly critical of a number of practices followed by the company. Mr. Nelson got the young CPA to drop some and soften other recommendations. Two months after completion of the audit, Gordon Seemann joined the mortgage company as its Chief Financial Officer.

"Mr. Nelson, I don't understand what we are supposed to have done that was so bad. We have 6,000 employees and 4,000 agents and independents. We can't know what every one of those is doing all the time. How can they make us responsible for a few over enthusiastic sales types who went overboard?"

"Gordon, we are the worst kind of bad guys—fat cats with big salaries. Lansden would have convinced the jury that we deliberately set out to rip off old people, widows, and orphans. You and I know it wasn't that way. Right? Everyone was supposed to be working off the same forms. Everyone was using "stated income" so we could commit on the spot. If we hadn't gone along with it, we wouldn't have had any business. The competition didn't give us time to verify the income information. Like everybody else—we let the applicants fill in their income information on the application form. We take their word for it. The applicants swear to it. What are we supposed to do, call our customers liars and crooks? We had some bad apples like everyone else. Our jerk agent in that hick-town Nashville was one of them. Okay, so he told people what to put on the forms. They say he recruited refis—showed people how they could get some real spending money by borrowing more than their house was worth. Damn fools took the money and blew it—big ass vacations, gambling, or whatever. Hell, they just pissed it away! Then the buffoons could not afford the damn payments. And, that is supposed be our fault? How were we supposed to know that? Hell, we were, what, 1500 miles away in New York? We gave them the damn book. We told them to follow the damn thing. What the hell did they think we wrote those procedures for? We depend on people to follow our rules, right? If they don't, if they do bad things, then they are the jerks who should be hauled to court—sent to jail. Not us!"

"Mr. Nelson, Nashville wasn't the only place. A lot of that stuff was going on in Orange County, right? So why is Nashville such a big problem?"

"Gordon, the problem wasn't about Nashville. It was about that dead bastard, Lansden. He wasn't just some lawyer. He was a damn politician. That guy was trying to make a national name for himself. Hell, the man actually thought he could be the President. We are taking care of those Orange County problems. We're doing it quietly. That damn Lansden wasn't into doing things quietly. Nashville could have snowballed and taken us down. Lansden wanted blood—ours!

It is different now. The "great litigator" is dead—no more gravy train for the other partners in his law firm. Lansden's firm is going to have their hands full trying to fill his shoes. Hell, they can't do it! H.T. Lansden was a busy man—had a zillion balls in the air. With Lansden out of the picture, we can head this thing off before it does snowball, or worse, lead to a class action suit. We need to get to the client and settle—and get them to sign a non-disclosure agreement. We make them an offer they can't refuse, but one we can afford."

"I wish I shared your optimism, Mr. Nelson. The law firm may not roll over on this. What if they want to hold out for a mega jury verdict?"

"They don't have any reason to go big time with this. It was Lansden's ambition that was driving this. They are smarter than that. They know how long a court case would take. We would appeal. If we slow-walked things, it would be years before the client or the law firm would see one damn penny. Hell, the publicity would destroy us anyway, and their jury award would be worthless. Lansden didn't give a shit about the money. A settlement will immediately put money in the firm's bank account. It will be one less of Lansden's hot potatoes that the firm has to deal with. And Lansden's death may have them worrying about their own hides. The timing is right. It always pays to take advantage of someone else's misery."

"Anything I can do to help, Mr. Nelson?"

"Gordon, it wouldn't hurt to have a friend inside Lansden's law firm—someone who keeps us posted—maybe even in a position to encourage the Fenios to accept the settlement."

"We may have an inside man—someone we have been cultivating, just in case. He contacted us about a job—a big salary position in our legal department, Assistant General Counsel. He hinted that he might be able to help us out with the Fenio case. I've been stringing him along."

"Who is it?"

"His name is Bill Maxwell."

"How far down the ladder is he?"

"He claims he is one of three senior associates they have talked to about moving to partner level."

Nelson expressed his skepticism, "Wouldn't that kind of make our job less attractive to him?"

"The firm has a funny compensation system. I won't bore you with the details, but according to Maxwell the only thing being a partner gets you in that firm is personal liability for the firm's debt and for malpractice claims."

"See what you can get out of him. Who is going to take over the Fenio case? Is there any chance he can get involved through his end—help us get this thing settled

ASAP? You can tell him it would make the Assistant General Counsel job his. Hell, tell him it will be Vice President and Assistant General Counsel."

"Will do."

"Yep, Gordon, you should celebrate. It is a good day. The Wicked Barrister is dead, or maybe I should say the Bastard is dead—and good riddance to him!"

"Mr. Nelson, you seem a little too happy about this."

"You bet your ass, I'm happy!"

"I mean, we didn't have anything to do with this, did we?"

Keith Nelson laughed. "Why Gordon, how can you ask such a thing? I'm just the Good Bastard whose house fell on the Bad Bastard. It was an act of God." He looked up at the ceiling, raised his hands, and laughed as he exclaimed, "Thank you, God!"

Then Nelson stopped laughing and focused on Seemann. "And you should thank God too, Gordon. If Lansden had had his way, your stock options would be worthless. You would be out of a job—penniless. The only job you could get is as a shoe salesman, or worse, a mattress salesman. Jail might have even looked good to you—a roof over your head and three squares a day. Count your blessings, my son, and don't question good fortune when it comes your way. Just keep thinking—Ding Dong! The Wicked Barrister is dead!"

The Claret Murders
Copyright © 2012 M. Thomas Collins

Chapter 1

Howard J. Taylor, the Old Man

It was 10:00 a.m. Christmas Day, 1959. The sun was shining brightly and it was 55 degrees—unusually warm for that time of year. The sun made it seem even warmer.

Hidden by a dense hedge of yews, a masonry wall guarded the gray stone mansion two hundred yards off Hillsboro Road. A stone drive curved gracefully from the road to the house. Its loose brown gravel added a casual country estate feeling. It would have been inviting except for the heavy wrought iron gate—a gate that both protected and imprisoned the old man inside.

Sitting in a wheelchair, Howard J. Taylor peered through the glass French doors that opened onto the second-floor front veranda. Seventy-two years had not treated him kindly. Beaten down by a series of small strokes and laboring for every breath due to degenerative heart disease, he was more like a man of ninety. He dressed the same every morning, now with the help of his attendant, William Walker, who the old man called his "black man." Taylor wore the uniform of a Southern gentleman banker of his generation—gray suit and vest. He wore Adler Cap-Toe shoes, their fine black leather polished to a mirror-like finish. His tie was Mogador silk—classic

British stripe, navy blue and burgundy red with a fine yellow line between the wider stripes. Prepared for the walk around the garden he could no longer make, he wore a round flat-topped straw hat. His folded hands rested on the silver handle of an alabaster cane set between his legs, ready if he should try to free himself from the wheelchair. He sat and stared like a sentinel—waiting for visitors or ready to repel them. The truth is, his motive was a little of both.

Howard Taylor had been a lawyer, a banker, and the owner of an investment firm. He had money when the Depression hit and used it to buy stocks and land as prices plummeted. He took no prisoners. He made his money off the pain and sorrow of others. Some fought back—hired lawyers and sued Taylor to recover foreclosed property or for investments that went bad. He slowly acquired an intense hatred for lawyers. In Taylor's words: "Lawyers are a bunch of crooks and liars."

In the very middle of the Depression, he built the mansion that later became his lonely prison. Then World War II came. He was too old for the draft. The war ended. The economy boomed and so did his wealth. His wife had loved him. She had looked past his three indiscretions during their forty years together. The marriage produced four children he hardly knew. There was a love child or what might more appropriately be called an "inconvenient consequence" of a night of heavy drinking and a quickie with a bosomy young black girl in his employment. He had chanced upon her that night and she had served his purposes. He provided financially through the child's college years but would have nothing else to do with her.

As for the mother, she remained on his domestic staff, but he never showed the slightest bit of interest in her—he never had any.

Howard Taylor's legitimate children went their separate ways and were too busy to return home even during their mother's brief illness preceding her death in 1957. After his wife's death, he heard from the children but only when they wanted money. With their mother no longer available, they had to ask him directly. He turned them away—the way they had turned their backs on his dying wife, on their own mother.

While he was an active part of the Nashville business community, he thought he was an important man—even a great man. There were the yes-men and yes-women on his payroll, who smiled and said good morning, laughed at his infrequent jokes, and were quick to praise his wisdom and successes. There were his business peers for whom he had held the purse strings to the funds they needed to run their businesses. Then things changed.

His local investment firm was the first to be acquired. His Nashville bank merged with a large national chain a year later. Within a year, the new owners forced the old man out of both companies he had started from nothing and built into financial successes. After the mergers he was even richer, but he no longer held sway over the lives of others. His former employees and business peers soon forgot him. Their allegiance shifted to the new owners.

The old man became increasingly bitter. The occasional visitors at the gate, usually members of the church he no longer attended, were rebuffed and sent away. He refused the infrequent telephone calls from his ungrateful children so they soon stopped calling. Aside from reluctant contact with the man who managed his financial affairs and his growing dependence on William Walker and William's wife, Mildred, the old man had cut himself off from human connection.

The Walkers, in their early forties, and the younger cook lived in the caretaker's bunkhouse. It was the Walkers who dealt with the outside world when it came to the house and grounds. They managed the landscapers, repairmen, butcher, and grocer. They protected Taylor from mingling with the masses for the necessities of everyday life. Any kindness within Howard J. Taylor was reserved for William and Mildred. He had none for the other domestics. He made no allowances for their personal needs nor for holidays, including Christmas. On this Christmas Eve, he had been particularly vile to his cook. The poor woman had found the courage to speak directly to him—to beg him for a little time off on Christmas Day to be with the child in her sister's care—*her* child from *his* seed!

How could I have let that monster have me that night? she asked herself over and over. The encounter had left her feeling dirty. But she knew the answer. She had been only sixteen and he was her master. There was nothing else she could have done. But times had changed. She wasn't sixteen anymore. She was no longer afraid. She loved her child, but as for the monster who fathered it—she was filled with hate.

— ∫ —

Robert Callaway, the man who handled Taylor's financial affairs, was almost as old as Taylor himself. Callaway had worked for Taylor at the investment firm before Taylor sold it. When the new owners forced him out, Taylor hired Callaway to handle his financial affairs. Callaway was honest and unflinchingly loyal. Taylor made sure Callaway was well taken care of financially. Callaway became wealthy in his own right just by mirroring, albeit on a much smaller level, Taylor's investments. It was Callaway who dealt with the hated lawyers and despised accountants. Callaway was the only visitor admitted to the mansion—and that occurred only when the old man's signature was required.

Year after year, Callaway pushed the old man to have a will prepared. Year after year, motivated by his loathing of lawyers and bitterness toward his ungrateful children, Taylor refused. Finally, irritated by Callaway's persistence, he took pen in hand. As Callaway watched, Taylor wrote a few sentences. Then he signed, dated, and presented Callaway the paper, which read as follows:

> *Being of sound mind and body I write this, my first, last, and only will:*
>
> *The house I live in and its grounds, including all outbuildings, furnishings, equipment, and personal property of every kind located in my house and on said grounds, shall be retained intact for the benefit of William and Mildred Walker as long as either shall live and continue to occupy the caretaker's cottage. The executor of my will shall provide for*

the preservation of said property and provide William and/or Mildred Walker with an income adequate for each to live in comfort and shall provide for the medical needs of each as long as they shall live. As for the rest of my affairs, I shall not aid my heirs in their lust for my wealth; I leave that to the courts and lying lawyers to sort out.

June 2, 1956
Signed: Howard J. Taylor

— ƒ —

William came and got the old man for his lunch. Mildred had ordered the cook to prepare his favorite—homemade beef stew with well cooked meat and vegetables soft enough for the old man's failing gums and loose teeth. Mildred smiled at him as she served the soup. She then carefully placed on the table a tall glass of buttermilk and a slice of hot cornbread just removed from an iron skillet. He dipped the cornbread—some in the soup and some in the buttermilk. As the finale to his Christmas lunch, Mildred brought in a small plate of soft French cheese.

At William's bidding, the cook retrieved a bottle of twelve-year-old claret from the butler's pantry. The wine was first opened the night before—on Christmas Eve. The old man called it his "good stuff." He reserved this wine for himself. The cook did not smile as she poured him an ample glass. Without a word, she returned to the kitchen, taking the bottle and its unpoured contents with her.

After lunch William took Taylor to his room for his routine midday nap. William always woke him at 3:00 p.m., and then the old man would resume his position as sentry. At three o'clock on this Christmas afternoon, William could not wake him—the old man was dead. No one had come to the gate—no one to be welcomed or repelled.

About Tom Collins
Author, Entrepreneur, and Epicurean

Photograph by John Guide

The London-based publication *Citytech* called him an "outstanding individual and visionary" when M. Thomas (Tom) Collins was named as one of the Top 100 Global Tech Leaders in the legal community. Tom Collins, as he prefers to be called, is also the recipient of the Lifetime Achievement Award from the US Publication *Law Technology News* for his contribution to the use of technology in the legal community. Although now retired from the commercial world, he continues to write and speak on the subject of leadership and management while penning his Mark Rollins adventure series of mysteries.

www.tomcollinsauthor.com

Tom Collins is available for selected readings and lectures. To inquire about a possible appearance, contact PLA Media at 615-327-0100 or info@plamedia.com.

APPENDIX
THE ADDICTION PROCESS AND DRUG NAMES USED IN *DIVERSION*

There are two roads to addiction. One is the desire for pleasure. The other is relief from physical pain. In either case, the first few times, the user gets a feeling of improved well-being from consuming opiate drugs like heroin, morphine, codeine, and Hydrocodone. The desire to repeat that feeling leads to taking more of the drug. Each time the feeling of well-being, even euphoria, becomes less achievable and is replaced by "the black dog" (depression, pain, a feeling of unwellness) when the individual is not under the influence of a sufficient dose of their drug. This is the point of addiction, when the individual "just wants to feel good again."

The addiction process occurs as opiates rewire the brain to shut off the body's natural production of endorphins. Endorphins are the chemicals produced by the brain that transmit electrical signals within the nervous system to regulate feelings of pain. More endorphins lead to feelings of wellness, warmth, even euphoria, and they modulate appetite, release of sex hormones, and enhance our immune response.

The good feeling is the result of opiates flooding the body with endorphins, many times more than the body produces naturally. That excess of endorphins tricks the brain into shutting down its own endorphin production. When the brain throws that switch to the off position, seeking pleasure through drugs turns instead to avoiding pain. Taking more and more of the drug is the only way to make up for the lost endorphins. Without the drug, the individual suffers.

Heroin and cocaine are illegal, period. But pain medications like OxyContin, Percocet, and Fentanyl, for example, are both—legal and illegal. Once they are diverted to the illegal world they shed their medical and brand names for street slang. In *Diversion* both medical names and street slang are used.

Drug names appearing in *Diversion*:

- 40-Bar: street name for a 40mg OxyContin pill.

- 512s: street name for a white, round Percocet pill with a 512 imprint that contains 325mg of Acetaminophen and 5mg of oxycodone.

- 80s: street name for an 80mg OxyContin pill.

- Bennies: slang for the drug Benzedrine, a stimulant like methamphetamine.

- Blues: street name for Roxicodone, an instant release oxycodone tablet in either 15mg or 30mg.

- Carisoprodol (aka Soma): a muscle relaxer that blocks pain sensations between the nerves and the brain. It produces all the effects associated with barbiturates.

- Cotton: often used on the street to refer to cocaine, heroin, or morphine— collectively the Cotton Brothers.

- Fentanyl: a synthetic opioid similar to morphine but 50 to 100 times more potent. It is also sold under the trade names Actiq, Duragesic, and Sublimaze. On the street, fentanyl or fentanyl-laced heroin has many colorful names including Apache, China Girl, China White, Dance, Tango, Fever, Friend, Goodfella, Jackpot, Murder 8, and TNT.

- Goofballs: slang for Barbiturates such as phenobarbital, secobarbital, and derivatives of barbituric acid.

- Go-pills: slang for drugs issued by the military to enable soldiers and pilots to remain awake for extended periods. In addition to traditional amphetamines, go-pills can include new stimulants such as modafinil (ProVigil). On the street, equivalent pills would be called uppers or speed.

- Heroin: an opioid made from morphine. It can be a white or brown powder, or black tar. Street names for heroin include dope, horse, junk, and smack. It is injected, snorted, or smoked.

- Holy Trinity: three pills taken together—OxyContin, Xanax, and Soma or Carisoprodol. Their Immediate-release formulations have the rapid onset that abusers seek.

- Hydrocodone: also known as dihydrocodeinone. Hydrocodone is a semi-synthetic opioid synthesized from codeine. It is usually formulated as a combination pill that includes acetaminophen and is sold under the trade names Vicodin, Norco, and Lortab.

- Lortabs: a brand name for a painkiller combining hydrocodone and acetaminophen. Available in three strengths of hydrocodone—5mg, 7.5mg, and 10mg.

- Methamphetamine: a powerful stimulant, chemically like amphetamine, used to treat ADHD and narcolepsy. Methamphetamine is a white, bitter-tasting powder or a pill. Crystal methamphetamine looks like glass fragments or shiny, bluish-white rocks. Other common names for methamphetamine include chalk, crank, crystal, ice, meth, and speed.

- Morphine: a pain medication of the opiate type found naturally in many plants and animals. It can be given by mouth, by injection, or rectally and has a high potential for addiction and abuse.

- Mushroom: in the drug world, a group of fungi that contain the psychedelic compounds psilocybin, psilocin, and baeocystin. Common street terms include magic mushrooms and shrooms. They are used as a recreational drug whose effects can include euphoria, altered thinking processes, closed and open-eye visuals, synesthesia, an altered sense of time, and spiritual experiences.

- O-Bombs: one of the street names for Opana.

- Opana: To combat abuse of OxyContin, its maker changed the formula of OxyContin tablets to make the pills more difficult to crush. That led to an increased popularity of Opana. Opana is the brand name for oxymorphone hydrochloride, a narcotic painkiller similar to morphine. It is like OxyContin except twice as strong. The six-sided Opana pills go by many street names including pink lady, pink heaven, stop signs, octagons and O-Bombs. Opana has a shorter high than OxyContin, which makes it more addictive since additional drugs are required to maintain the desired level of euphoria.

- Oxy: street name for OxyContin.

- Oxycodone: While Oxycodone is also a semisynthetic opioid, it is considered the lesser of two evils compared to OxyContin because it is usually combined with other medications like ibuprofen or Tylenol. On the other hand, the accompanying acetaminophen that it is combined with is likely to lead acute liver failure for the long-term user.

- OxyContin: considered the most abused opioid in the country. It is a drug of choice for many prescription addicts. OxyContin is frequently called "hillbilly heroin." It reacts on the nervous system like heroin or opium; thus, it is used as a substitute for, or supplement to, street opiates like heroin. OxyContin contains a pure concentration of oxycodone and the formulation makes the drug strong and intensely addictive.

- Percocet: a combination of acetaminophen and oxycodone. Oxycodone is an opioid pain medication. Acetaminophen increases the effects of oxycodone. The portion of Percocet that is oxycodone is a relatively small 5mg, 7.5mg, and 10mg compared to some alternative sources of Oxycodone.

- Percs: street name for Percocet.

- Roxi: street name for Roxidone.

- Roxidone: an oxycodone hydrochloride tablet, an opioid analgesic, available in 5mg, 15mg, and 30mg strengths. The 5mg, 15mg, and 30mg tablets contain the equivalent of 4.6mg, 13.5mg and 27.0mg, respectively, of oxycodone free base; thus, for the addict Roxidone delivers a higher dose than Percocet.

- Stop Signs: one of the street names for Opana, a six-sided pill.

- Tramadol: acts on the central nervous system to relieve pain much like morphine, hydrocodone, and oxycodone. While technically not a narcotic, it is nevertheless a Schedule IV substance within the United States under the Controlled Substance Act. When used for a long time it is habit-forming with side effects like true opioids if the user goes off the medication.

- Vicodin: Like Percocet, Vicodin is a Hydrocodone/acetaminophen combination formula. It is indicated for relief of moderate to severe pain of acute, chronic, or postoperative types. Hydrocodone diversion and recreational use has escalated in recent years. As with Percocet, Vicodin is available in strengths of 5mg, 7.5mg and 10mg.

- Vics: street name for Vicodin

- Xanax: Alprazolam, trade name Xanax, is a potent, short-acting anxiolytic of the benzodiazepine class drug. It is used for the treatment of anxiety disorders, especially of panic disorder, and for treatment of generalized anxiety disorder. It has anxiolytic, sedative, muscle relaxant, anticonvulsant, amnestic, and antidepressant properties.